P9-CFV-771

The War in Georgia

Jerrie Oughton

Houghton Mifflin Company
Boston 1997

For information about this and other Houghton Mifflin
trade and reference books and multimedia products, visit
The Bookstore at Houghton Mifflin on the World Wide
Web at http://www.hmco.com/trade/.

The text of this book is set in 13 point Bembo.

Library of Congress Cataloging-in-Publication Data
Oughton, Jerrie.
The war in Georgia / by Jerrie Oughton.
p.   cm.
Summary: Living in Georgia during World War II,
thirteen-year-old Shanta sometimes feels that her
family and neighborhood are more hopeless battlefields
than those in foreign lands.
ISBN 0-395-81568-1
[1. Neighborhood — Fiction. 2. Family life — Fiction.
3. War — Fiction. 4. World War, 1939-1945 —
United States — Fiction.]   I. Title.
PZ7.0897War   1997
[Fic] — dc20   96-22029   CIP   AC

Printed in the United States of America

BP   10   9   8   7   6   5   4   3   2   1

For Mary Frances Johnson Preston,
Edwin Smith Preston, Sr.,
Althea Morgan Johnson,
and
Nym Hurt Johnson,
who once, long ago, taught me joy.

"Oh, but war's not for children — it's for men."

"Now we are digging almost down to China.
My dears, my dears, you thought that — we all thought it.
So your mistake was ours. Haven't you heard, though,
About the ships where war has found them out
At sea, about the towns where war has come
Through opening clouds at night with droning speed
Further o'erhead than all but stars and angels —
And children in the ships and in the towns?
Haven't you heard what we have lived to learn?
Nothing so new — something we had forgotten:
War is for everyone, for children, too."

— from *The Bonfire* by Robert Frost

Prologue

All these years later I still miss her. My grandmother. Miss her skin, soft, like a petunia petal. Her voice cranking on its edge, yet rounded by Georgia's way of saying words, ignoring r's. Seems like yesterday she'd come to the back porch and hail me down from the mimosa tree. She and my Uncle Louie shaped my life. They were the only family I knew.

The missing takes such a strong hold sometimes I'm beside myself to do something with it. Finally I did. It was an unseasonably warm day in early March last year. I was on my lunch break. The gusts of spring's-coming air whipped at the bare trees, and my mind was once again full of Georgia springs. Red clay soil growing dogwoods to die for.

So, I sat right there in the car and wrote a letter to my grandmother. No matter she's been dead thirty years now. "Dear Grandmorgan," I wrote . . .

And I just flat out told her how I missed her and Louie. I mentioned some of the things I remembered: the magicians coming almost every night to visit; the neighbors; the hollyhocks at the back fence; Betsy Manikin; Mr. Hadley in his straw hat, gardening the field that started beside the house and reached on out to the back of the property, his mule and wagon parked at the street; the mimosa tree with its cool, high-up limbs where a person could watch the comings and goings of the back yards all up and down Clay Street.

I told her I even missed that scary summer of 1945, the last days of World War II — the summer the Wallings moved in across the street, when things, some old, some new, got out of hand, and were so painful I can't even remember it all yet. It comes back in pieces that fit together into a large puzzle picture. Even now, I told her in my letter, some of those pieces are still missing.

Sometimes, though, writing memories down helps bring them back in their fullness, in a new light. Sheds fresh insight into old memories.

1

Georgia didn't start out being a war zone. Because there was a war going on across the ocean, it was important there be peace somewhere in our lives. World War II had been going on for three years, now, and by this last year of the war it looked as though another war had begun to smoulder. Closer to home. Actually *at* home. In Atlanta. On Clay Street.

My Uncle Louie and Aunt Louray's love had been a bonfire in the beginning, warming the walls between our rooms in Grandmorgan's house. Their wedding afternoon they had run from the trolley stop at the corner to our house at 29 Clay Street, heads up in the pouring rain. Honey was born to them out of that hot love, and, little smiling person that she is, she has worked her way into everybody's heart.

"Mama, Mama," Honey calls, running through the dark interior of the house this April afternoon. "It's Shanta's birthday in one day. One . . . whole . . . day!"

Louray is in the kitchen, listening to the radio with everybody else. "Hush," she hisses at Honey. "Listen."

The radio has everybody's ear. ". . . in Warm Springs, Georgia, where he often went for relaxation. To repeat, President Franklin Delano Roosevelt has died of a massive cerebral hemorrhage."

It is the kitchen radio that is our window on the world. We've clocked the entire war through listening around the kitchen table.

"Hmm-mm-pf." Louray stands up. "He wasn't much of a president anyway, I always say."

My grandmother looks up at her, startled.

"Well, if he'd been worth his salt he'd have stopped this war by now," Louray continues.

"Who'll be president now?" I ask, but direct the question to my Uncle Louie. Louray is too explosive. She could go off on a tangent that might involve people as far back in history as Moses or Noah.

"Harry S Truman," he says from where he sits in his wheelchair. Rheumatoid arthritis is bending and freezing him stiff. "He'll make us a good president, too," Louie adds.

"What!" Louray hops on that fast. "Truman is a crude bag of hot air. He's got . . ."

"He's got good intentions and common sense," my grandmother interrupts. "I believe he'll get us out of this war, though, Lord knows, FDR has tried."

Louray smiles, but there's nothing funny. It's one of those smiles that is a mask to hide behind where your real feelings lie. "That's just like you to say that."

Grandmorgan doesn't back down, though. "I should hope so. I wouldn't want to say anything out of character."

And now the only sound is people breathing and the radio. I may just be thirteen tomorrow (not that anybody will celebrate but me), but I can tell from where I sit that the seeds of war that have been sown during these past six years Louie and Louray have been married . . . those seeds are growing right along.

Louray shoots Louie a look that says she hates us all. *Yes,* I think, *the seeds may be there in the dark still, but they are making small movements toward the light.*

"Shanta?" Honey catches my hand.

I look down at her.

She cups her hand and stands on tiptoe to whisper in my ear. "There's a truck across the street."

We leave the kitchen and head out front to see what this afternoon holds for Clay Street.

Mr. and Mrs. Spindell, who have lived across the street since before I came to Clay Street, are moving out, lock, stock, and barrel. Honey and I watch from the street curb. It takes all afternoon, and after a while, she gets bored.

"Let's water the hollyhocks," she says.

There aren't any hollyhocks this early in the spring, but jonquils are everywhere. The driveway is a flat, gray runway with yellow jonquils, like lights up and down each side.

We drag the hose out, and I take the first turn to show Honey how to aim the heavy stream next to the flowers, not right on them to beat them all down. I water on the side next to the Stewarts' house. Two maiden ladies live there on the other side of our driveway, and, though they're nice, they're mighty boxed in. Everything has to be just right. You'd think they take a pencil and draw on their hair of a morning it's so tight. And they wear high heels to garden in. I figure it gives them leverage when they're tugging weeds, with those two-inch heels sinking into the dirt, holding them in place.

I've just about finished my side of the driveway, down near the street, when Ralph Edward Weathers puts in an appearance. This boy was hatched with snakes is all I've got to say. I'm in school with him nine months of the year so I figure I know him pretty well, and I can vouch — there's not a nice bone in his body.

"Hey," he calls, skidding his bike to a halt in the dirt and gravel at the bottom of our drive. "You look just like the Little Boy of Brussels, holding that hose!"

I get his reference. We saw a picture of that statue in school this year in art appreciation. Ralph Edward especially appreciated a statue of a little naked boy peeing.

"That really was down your alley, Ralph Edward," I call back. "I'll bet the sculptor thought of you when he made that statue."

I watch how he looks down the street like a smart answer would walk up and jump in his mouth. Wishing it would.

Miss Lelia Stewart comes out her porch door and teeters down the front steps in her heels. She's so intent on plucking limp jonquil blooms that she doesn't even speak.

"Well," Ralph Edward brays out, "at least I can stand up to do it. I don't have to squat."

I can't believe he said that.

Louray comes to the door at the side of our front porch. "Honey, it's time to come in and take your bath. We're going to church after supper."

"No!" Honey wails. "It's my turn with the hose. It's MY turn!" She's jumping up and down where she stands.

Louray doesn't like not minding. She pops off that porch like a cork out of a bottle and marches for the faucet to cut off the water. Seeing she's not going to get her turn, Honey throws one blue fit. She snatches the hose from me and sprays after Louray, trying to catch her and drown her, I guess.

Louray's too fast for her and runs out of reach. "Shanta!" she screeches, like it's all my fault.

Before I can grab it back, though, Honey swings around and gets me good. Not that it matters. Feels good actually. But, on the way she douses Miss Lelia Stewart, who's popped back up to see the commotion; I don't think it feels good to her.

It's amazing, really, what a stream of water can do to a hairdo. Miss Lelia suddenly has a fish face, her lips forming a circle, and her hair is standing straight back. And there's no way for her to escape because her heels have sunk her in like cleats on a football field.

Ralph Edward is still in the street, laughing. I look over. That preacher's boy is standing on the pedals so he can see Miss Lelia better, catching himself whenever the bike tilts to one side.

Honey couldn't have made a better move if she'd been coached. She takes the hose with both grubby little hands and turns it full on Ralph Edward. It almost knocks him off the bike. Wipes that smile right off his face, too. He's cussing and grappling with his bike. Finally he thinks he has it under control and wheels to escape. But the dirt under him is now nothing but mud, and he skids sideways, leveling out flat. It is so gratifying to watch him lie right down in the mud that Honey and I just stand and take it in. Even after Louray has cut the water, we're still watching, saving it up to remember. And I know, he'll make us pay for this. Probably all summer long. But right now I don't even care.

"What's that you said about squatting, Ralph Edward?" I ask loud and don't care who hears.

Mr. and Mrs. Spindell honk the truck horn to say goodbye and drive off toward Boulevard Drive. It's one of those times you never forget. Two friends leaving your life and your sworn enemy groveling in the mud at your feet. I know what bittersweet means.

The next day I'm still congratulating Honey on her perfect move with Ralph Edward. We laugh again as we cross the street and peer in the blank windows at the empty rooms of the Spindells' house. Finding the back door unlocked, we go on inside, but know we probably shouldn't.

"Wonder who'll come next?" Honey whispers.

"You don't have to whisper." My voice booms and echoes off the solemn, scarred walls.

We go into every room. Shutting the back door, we discover outside cellar stairs and creep down them into a damp, earthen-floored cell that repels you with its stench.

"Let's leave," Honey whines when I stop to look at a heavy metal chain, anchored to the stone wall. It gives the small room a rancid odor. Through a dirt-spattered glass pane, the afternoon sun glumly stops mid-room, refusing to reach for corners.

"Please," Honey whines.

We turn to leave. "Probably tied their dog down there in wet weather," I tell Honey, but can't shake that chain from my head. Its shortness, not more than five feet. Its heaviness like a ship's anchor chain.

But Honey is in such a hurry to leave, she stubs her toe on the bottom step.

"Oh-h-h-h," she wails. Then kicking the step with her other foot, she screams, "You damn stair!"

"What did you say?" I ask her. "Where did you learn that?"

"Daddy said it when he slipped with his crutch." Then she groans and squeezes her toe hard and hops up into the sunlight to get a better look.

"I don't care," I tell her, hot on her heels. "You can't say *damn*. You're too little."

"You just said it."

"I know. I'm big. You have to say *darn* or maybe *dern* if you're hurt bad. But you can't say *damn*."

"I'll say it if I want to. Mama . . ."

She is off like a shot. Doesn't even look before she darts across the street. I catch her by the arm at

the opposite curb. "You ran across that street without looking!"

"Mama!" Honey wails, twisting out of my grasp.

Louray balks the screen door wide and Honey
sails up the steps, grabbing her by the knees, screaming like I had decked her good.

"I can, too, say *damn*, can't I?"

Louray slashes her eyes from Honey to me coming up the steps. "You been teaching her bad words,
Shanta?"

Before I can open my mouth to explain, Louray
clamps me with guilt and sends me off for life.
"She's only five, Shanta. If I ever catch you teaching
Honey curse words, I'll take her so far away you'll
never see her again. Do you understand me?"

It is a wall Louray throws between us. Or maybe
just paints the invisible one that has been building
there for a long time, and now I can finally see it.
In my life I have never felt a moment this alone.
Even when I heard my parents had both been killed
in the automobile accident. I barely remember that.
Then I had been little and had Grandmorgan and
Louie. This is different. Everyone might believe
Louray. I, alone, know that it isn't true.

I just stand. Life is full of people who will read
you wrong but I have not bumped into one before.
Until Louray. Now I know I'll be the one to blame
if Louray yanks Honey out of our lives. Louray will
lay it to me and disappear forever.

2

As clear as though it were this morning, I remember the day America entered World War II. It was December 8th, 1941. The day before, Japanese bombers had parted the coils of mist over Diamond Head and said goodbye to the battleship *Arizona*. They said *Sayonara* to more than five thousand people before they left that day. My grandmother wore a black arm band in memory of those who had died the day before. We were at war.

The summers of the war Louie and I started listening to baseball games on the radio. Louray rocked Honey to sleep on the front porch and Louie and I sat in the living room. Most of the time it was just the two of us, but, now and then, some of his magician friends would stop by and listen with us. Sometimes we heard the New York Yankees. Sometimes the Brooklyn Dodgers. But more often than not it was the Atlanta Crackers.

"Will the Atlanta Crackers ever play in the World Series?" I asked Louie.

"Nope. Never. They belong to the Southern League. Just a farm team."

"Farmers?"

He laughed. "They are the guys who didn't make the cut. They're not in the majors. Only on a farm team."

"So they'll never play in the World Series?"

"Nope," he said. "Not unless one lucks out and moves up to the majors."

One summer Joe DiMaggio got a hit in fifty-six consecutive games and set a new major league record. And in the World Series that fall, the Yankees beat Brooklyn. The Atlanta Crackers, like Louie and me, probably listened to the Series on the radio. Not major league material.

My Uncle Louie wasn't eligible to be drafted into the military because arthritis was working him over good. He was walking with a cane in 1941. The person on our street who was drafted was Jimmy Piersey, across the street. Beginning the day Jimmy Piersey went to war, his mother never has set foot outside her door again. Not the whole war. Friends and neighbors run her errands and in she stays, like she is tending an important egg, not able to leave her nest until the egg hatches.

This spring of 1945, it seems a lot of people important to the war die. First there is Roosevelt. Next Ernie Pyle, a war correspondent whose column Louie reads in the newspaper every morning. Then Mussolini, the Italian version of Hitler. And finally Hitler himself, though nobody can find his body. That doesn't even count all the soldiers. No bad word on Jimmy Piersey, yet.

On a May Monday, when the new people move into the Spindells' old house, Mrs. Piersey is stationed at her front window almost all day. She watches better than anybody on the street. We all can keep an eye out from time to time. But Mrs. Piersey is the expert sentry, tending her egg and watching. It is her calling. Her career, along with the egg.

I'm sweeping the front walk, watching the truck that has pulled up across the street. It's parked in the driveway of the empty house next door to Mrs. Piersey. Now a car pulls in behind. The broom handle anchors me in place while I watch a whole family emerge from both vehicles. Maybe more than a family. Two men crawl out of the truck cab swigging on bottles of beer, undershirts stuck to their chests and backs with sweat. From the car a woman works her way out from behind the wheel. When she stands, it is easy to see why she had the seat pulled so far forward. Her head barely rises above the top of the car, she's so short.

From the other car doors come three girls and a boy. The boy and two of the girls are older than I am and one girl is about my own age, I guess. They stretch as though they've ridden for hours. The boy looks around the neighborhood, taking in Clay Street in a long sweep. When he comes to me he stops. I wave, wonder if he'll skip on over me and slide right on to Mr. Hadley's mule, parked with its wagon at the curb of the street. Mr. Hadley is working my grandmother's garden today and the mule waits like a chauffeur until his rider is ready to leave.

But no, the boy lifts a hand and waves back at me. It's a strange greeting, though. Sort of a gliding wave. Slow. Not quite correct, as waving goes.

The girls look to where he is waving and smile across at me. But that is all. The street could be the Atlantic Ocean flowing between two continents as far as it goes this morning. And maybe, in ways, it would be better for all of us standing there on that steaming May morning in 1945, if it were an uncrossable expanse instead of just twenty-seven feet of concrete with tar seams.

The woman, short as she is, commands their full respect and with her voice she jerks the attention of the yardful of family back to their morning's work, the unloading of the truck. And I watch as I sweep, not only my own front walk, but also the cracked and broken sidewalk out front by the street so I can legitimately stay and take it all in. I drag out the sweeping for as long as I can, but unloading the truck takes the full morning and into the afternoon.

Grandmorgan comes out early to water the petunias. I notice that she has shampooed her long gray hair and wrapped it, still wet, in a roll around the slim elastic band she always wears around her head. Not a stray hair moves in the morning breeze.

Louie says my daddy looked like my grandmother, had her eyes. It's hard to picture it, though. I don't remember my mother and daddy. When they were killed, I was two and came to live here on Clay Street. I find myself thinking about my parents more and more, the older I get. Their pictures tell me nothing I want to know. Not about my real family. Not how my daddy might have let me ride piggyback and my mother might have rocked me to sleep in a chair right on Grandmorgan's front porch. The very place I pass every day of my life. I watch Grandmorgan and wish I knew more.

Mrs. Piersey leans out her porch door to shake a rag rug, and Grandmorgan waves across to her, says, "I'll be over later with a salad I'm fixing for you, Lucille." Mrs. Piersey nods and goes back in.

Next door to our house, McGolphin, who leaves for work five mornings a week, backs his car out of his driveway and takes off down the street, leaving a smoke signature trailing behind him. Grandmorgan always refers to McGolphin as "the best neighbor a body ever had." This morning, she waves to him while she says it now, then she pauses to watch the goings-on across the street. "New people," she says to me, nodding her head toward the truck being unloaded.

I smile in answer and keep sweeping.

Mr. Hadley finishes his morning gardening of Grandmorgan's garden plot and drives the mule down the street. I leave off sweeping and Uncle Louie has two customers come and go before the truck has yielded its full load to the empty house. These are watch-repair customers, since that is what Louie does these days to earn a living. In our front lawn, all fifteen feet of it, bank included, there hangs a small wooden clock. "Does it tell time?" Honey asks every day of her life. Then, "Why doesn't it tell time?" She is five and asking questions is her career.

"Because," I tell her this morning as we sit eating our split halves of a banana Popsicle on the front porch steps so we can keep an eye on the moving-in across the street, "it's a sign. A advertisement." Usually, I merely say, "Because," or "Go ask your mama." Today it is a good reason to extend my front yard watching of the moving-in.

"Your daddy fixes watches and jewelry. See. It

says his name. Instead of numbers it has the letters of his name. L—O—U—I—E—space—M—O—R—G—A—N. That lets people know what house on Clay Street he lives at.

"And," I add, delighting in this part because it is so wonderfully odd, "if it's five minutes after five, on Louie's clock it's O—after—space."

"Does it work?"

"No, I told you. It's just a sign."

"Why?" Honey asks, catching a cold drip with her tongue before it has a chance to hit the cement beneath.

"Why what?"

"Why does my daddy fix watches?"

I could say, because they're broken. Or, going for a more complicated answer, because arthritis has crippled all but his hands and arms and it's what he can do. Not what he *wants* to do, but what he *can* do. I choose the latter.

"What does he want to do?"

Lord, she digests questions from the food she eats. I am sure of it. Honey never grows much. Is still small for five, frail. What she eats, egg whites (never the yolks), Popsicles, and other random bites of vegetables and meat all go to make her hair glorious and to whatever part of the brain manufactures questions. I envy her hair more than anything. It is the color of honey and hangs in waves. The name

16

was perfect before we even knew what she'd look like. Even Louray isn't as pretty as Honey.

"You know your daddy's friends that come some evenings?"

She nods and glances across the street to watch a large divan leave the truck and make its tortuous way up the steps and in the door, driven by all four children.

"The visitors are magicians. That's what Louie was before he came down with the arthritis. He was studying to be an accountant in the daytime so he could be a magician in the evenings and on the weekends. If he could have stuck with it long enough, he probably would have been a professional magician full time."

Honey slurps and doesn't answer with another question. I think we have moved on and am relieved. Too soon, however. It has just taken longer to form the next one.

"Couldn't his magician friends make him well again?"

I look at her. "There's a difference between magic and healing. Magic can pull an egg out of your ear, not rheumatoid arthritis from your daddy's joints."

Silence. Somewhere overhead a plane drones but it's too glaring a sky to try to track it. Honey has just pulled her lips together for her favorite word, *why,* when across the street a sharp crash splinters the quiet. A moment shorter than a rest in a piece of music follows. Then a guttural voice fuses the quiet into round, splattering words, some of which our grandmother would have rallied into action over. Words she would have flattened even grown people for using.

We watch as the taller man strides angrily toward the boy. There, on the front walk at the boy's feet, lies what is left of a lamp. Pieces of china stand cupped like petunias blooming in a flower border, the lampshade rolling slowly toward a stopping place of its own.

I have never liked to watch arguments. They can sour a whole day. This isn't really that, though, an argument. It is a one-sided torrent. A fire pouring into the head of the boy standing over the broken lamp. And the whole yardful of people have come to a standstill, like their energies have to be pooled toward this fire blazing there in their new front yard.

Watching isn't easy. Honey's sticky hand finds its way inside mine.

The boy stands rigid, silent as the telephone pole nearby. That's where the lampshade finally comes to rest. And, when the man has given out of words, he stoops to snatch up the lampshade and sends it from one hand to the other in silent tension. Finally he turns and carries the shade inside.

18

The people standing in the yard make small movements to begin their lives again, but the boy has turned to stone. Finally his mother comes and in low tones must say, "Pick up the pieces," because he kneels to do it and the pieces he picks up are from the china lamp. After she leaves to go inside and rearrange a house minus one lamp, his sisters come to pick up the pieces of the boy. But only after she has gone inside. And then it's hard, and I quit watching because I have never seen a boy big enough to be a man cry.

"Come on," I tell Honey, getting up, "let's go inside. Maybe Louie'll do some card fans for us."

Grandmorgan's house always smells like boiling cabbage and onions. It's dark, the farther in you go, and holds the heaviness in there that rainy days hold. We go down the long shadowy hall in the heart of the house and wash sticky Popsicle off our hands, then head back to the front of the house to Louie and Louray's bedroom/watch shop where sunshine streams in through the open porch door.

Honey and I do everything together. Even though she's eight years younger, she's the only person on the street to play with if you don't count Ralph Edward Weathers, two houses down on our side. I'd rather skip playing altogether than play with that excuse for a boy.

"Daddy, Daddy." Honey dances around Louie's wheelchair in her excitement.

"Hey, Punkin. Slow down a minute. What's up?"

He's leaning over the high watch-repair table, with his mouth held in such a way as to blow his breath straight down, past his chin, missing the table entirely.

"Why're you holding your mouth funny?" Honey asks, standing on tiptoe to try to see what he's working on.

He sits back and turns his whole upper torso slightly, since his neck is paralyzed. "So I won't blow the brains out of Mrs. Smithwick's watch," he says, looking at Honey. "That's why."

"Brains!" I say. "I didn't know watches had brains."

"Mrs. Smithwick's does," Louie tells me, a smile playing at the corner of his mouth.

"I'll blow her brains all across the room," Honey threatens gleefully.

Louie pops a glass cup over Mrs. Smithwick's watch and slides the work pad, watch and all, toward the back of the table, away from Honey, who is gathering in the biggest breath of all time. Before she can release it, Louie says, "I fixed that, didn't I?"

She laughs and the breath falls to pieces.

"Watch your tootsies," Louie warns, as he wheels his chair back and then to the right so he can face us. "Let's see now," he says, "you wanted me to pull a rabbit out of a hat . . ."

"No, no! We want card fans."

"Oh, I see," he says. "You want to see my hard hands." He holds his hands out for us to view.

"NO!" Honey screeches, smacking him on the hand. "You know what we want, Daddy."

Louie opens a drawer of his worktable and pulls out a deck of cards. He flips open the end of the box and shakes them out in one quick move of his hand. I love to watch Louie touch cards. He is really a professional in his card handling and proves it with every move.

Flourishing one hand, he cups the deck in the palm of his left hand and slips them into position. Smooth as butter, he takes the top of a fingernail and fans them into a perfect fan. Each card an eighth of an inch from the one in front.

"Wow!" Honey is fascinated. "Fan me, Daddy."

Louie fans her face, showing us the front and the back of the fan.

Louray comes through the room carrying a small stack of Honey's clean clothes she has folded.

"See, Mama," Honey calls, but Louray keeps on to Honey's and my room. Card fans no longer fascinate her, I guess. She's probably seen enough in her six years with Louie. As for me, I don't think I'll ever get tired of watching Louie circle cards to perfection. It's a gift, I figure. A talent. Not everybody can do it. Actually, very few people can do it. Louie is the only person I've ever met who could pull a perfect fan from an ordinary deck of cards.

That evening, long after the lights in the newly filled house across the street make lit rectangles out of the windows, that evening is when the arthritis strikes a bad blow to Louie. Unfortunately, there are no visiting magicians. Not when it happens. They have come and gone and Grandmorgan has turned off the porch light. First, has put her change for the breadman beneath the board on the ledge, and her empty milk bottle in the metal milk box. Then snaps off the light to say visiting hours are over. No more magicians tonight.

Louie is taking a bath when he just freezes stiff, right there in the tub. In a bathroom from which scents of talc and Airwick deodorizer seep out from around the closed door and on down the hall. Louray is putting back in her metal curlers so her hair will look formed and perfect in eight hours. And over in the bathtub, Louie just can't get back up. Not with Louray's help. Not with Grandmorgan pulling up on the other arm either.

"No, Shanta," Grandmorgan says fast to me as I stand at the open door, wanting to help but not knowing how. "No. You can't see a naked man. You're not old enough."

I back away, knowing full well what a naked man looks like. I don't have to see Uncle Louie to know that. Michelangelo had shown me David in all his bare glory. Just this year had shown a whole giggling class of sixth graders. A naked man is nothing much. Just skin and hair and an extra part that gives him the difference.

"Run next door to McGolphin. Tell him, come quick! Tell him Uncle Louie was taking a bath and can't lift himself outten the tub. Tell him he's stuck!" Grandmorgan's voice is quick and short. I've not heard this voice before. Grandmorgan flared up now and then, but this is different. Scared, not mad.

McGolphin is barefoot and in his sleeveless T-shirt, with a toothpick still working on supper shreds. But he comes without even shoes. And, being big, McGolphin lifts up Louie and, wrapping him in a towel so his nakedness won't embarrass him, carries him in his arms all the way down the long hall to his and Louray's room. And there, amid the small glass cups turned over top of ticking watches hospitalized in the care of Louie, across the room from the cabinet housing rope and rabbit-in-the-hat magic, McGolphin gently lowers my Uncle Louie to the waiting, spread-open covers of the antique bed. He makes sure, too, that Louie is comfortable before he stands back tall.

There are two carved cuckoo clocks, one on either side of the head of the antique bed. Silent, since they are carved, not real. They guard Louie this first night of the seven years he will lie in that room with his legs totally paralyzed by arthritis. They guard him well as we all enter into a war zone that none of us will ever forget. And the first casualty? Honey, with Louray snatching her from our home, from our lives.

Tomorrow will be V–E day. Western Europe will be free. At last the Allied troops will have conquered the axis powers. In less than a month, Louray Morgan will take a big step. She will set herself free from 29 Clay Street and all that it holds for her.

In war there are those who fight and die, the innocents who get hurt, and then there are those who live to tell about it. I'm not sure yet which role is mine.

3

I watch and wonder how someone closer than a sister can begin to inch away. It isn't something I can put a finger on. Or name the day it started. But comparing one year with the next, things have been growing cold, not hot and exciting. Not funny and hectic as they had promised. No longer faces up in rainstorms but withdrawal and apartness, from me and Grandmorgan and mostly from Louie. Then, for the first time, I find out Grandmorgan is feeling the same way.

"Now she's a pretty girl. I'll give her that," I hear her tell our neighbor, Finn McGolphin, one evening. Grandmorgan has crossed to the fence where they visit now and then. McGolphin loves to lean

25

on the fence and rile her, "get her going," he calls it. I figure it is McGolphin's hobby since he's too old to chase after deer, fish, or women.

"She's just not one to do much. After she comes home from work, she prefers to dry her nails and read magazines," Grandmorgan tells him.

"She don't help you cook? Great god! You're nearly eighty years old here . . ."

"What!" Grandmorgan squawks like a hen. "Eighty years old! I'm nowhere near eighty."

McGolphin chuckles. Has intended to get a rise out of her.

"And," Grandmorgan adds, calming again to her subject, "I don't expect her to come in from work and jump into housekeeping, or even visiting for that matter. But I do keep after Honey all day and she's a handful. By the time Louray hits the door . . ."

"Be nice if she'd help you cook," McGolphin offers.

Grandmorgan shakes her head and studies the corn stalks rowed up in the red dirt.

"Clean?"

She shakes her head again, never leaving the corn with her eyes.

"Wash clothes?"

Another head shake. "Only folds their personal things . . . and then I have to ask."

"Well good night, Morgan. She ain't nothing but a damned house guest!"

Grandmorgan's eyes leave the green growing corn and rise to McGolphin's. "At least a house guest would converse."

"She don't talk?"

Grandmorgan doesn't even bother to shake her head.

"To Louie?"

"Oh well, I guess she talks to him. And to Honey. But to me and Shanta — nothing."

"Is this a recent development?" McGolphin props one foot on the backside of the fence. I watch and listen from where I'm hidden up in the mimosa tree.

"Been like this for several years. And I know it's hard for two women to live together in a house. I'll grant you that . . ."

"Did it begin about the time Louie started coming down with the arthur-ritus?" McGolphin interrupts to ask.

"Maybe."

I was eight when Louie complained of his joints aching. All the time. The doctor told him he suspected arthritis. The bad kind. No matter what pills the pharmacy delivered to our door, nothing helped with the pain. It swallowed him, and we would hear him moaning from somewhere inside the pain.

Then the swelling began and the stiffness. It just crawled through Louie's legs and back like a poison and bent the joints, froze them. He did force his head back so he looked up, not drawn down to his chest like some people.

"At least my arms and hands are free," he had said to us. And it was true. Like two free souls, standing outside a prison fence watching trapped people, his arms helped him walk, first with a cane, then crutches, helped him fix watches and eat independently — all this in sight of the trapped prisoners, his legs.

"I think she stopped communicating about the time Louie dropped out of college entirely and went off to watch-repair school to learn a trade," Grandmorgan tells McGolphin, while she waves a hand holding a ripe tomato to fend off a fly that keeps buzzing her. "You know, she took Honey and went home to stay the three months while Louie was gone. When he got back, she came on across town to live here again, but she never really spoke to me from then on. There's no love lost between the Bentons and the Morgans anyway, and my theory is her parents poisoned her mind."

McGolphin turns his head to spit and then, wiping his chin with the back of his hand, says, "Mighty peculiar that you spend your days with a person who don't talk to you directly. Do you talk to her? I mean, hell, Morgan, ask her some di-rect questions. Make her talk to you. I would."

"I know you would, McGolphin. That's you, not me. I want her to *want* to, not *have* to." Grandmorgan stands, blind to the garden, searching inside for the one answer that will right the situation.

The argument erupts behind the closed doors of their bedroom. Louie has been stuck there now for almost a month and Louray has had free range of the whole of Atlanta. At least that's what she screams at him. I can't help but hear the words, standing in my next-door room.

"That's not what I said, Louray," Louie replies from where he lies in the bed.

"It's what you meant, though. Free range! Listen, I work every day. All right? I slave at that office alongside a group of unfriendly, catty girls who talk about me incessantly. But since it's essential that I work because my paycheck is what keeps this family afloat, I do it. I want Honey to have clothes that are pretty and toys. I want . . ."

All I can think about is how in love they started out. And how much Grandmorgan and I loved Louray back then.

"Here, Shanta," Louray had said the afternoon of their wedding day, "I want you to have my wedding hat to keep for always. To wear when you get married."

It was a blue cloche to match her blue velvet dress. Tiny glass beads looked like snail trackings all across it. Now it is high in my closet, saved for someday, I guess, but if marriage is like this, maybe saved for never.

Louray's voice breaks into my thoughts, and I decide it would be a good time to go check on Honey, who is taking a bath with her dolls. Listening to their arguments is unavoidable because of thin walls. At least I can leave, put distance between us. But before I can go, Louray's voice comes again, pounding through the closed door between our rooms, pulling me into this.

"Then I come home to a husband who does nothing but interrogate me. A mother-in-law who stonewalls me with her silence and an adolescent niece who is teaching my child to curse. I've had it! This is it! There is nothing for me here. Nothing!"

The door between our bedrooms suddenly bursts open and Louray glares at me where I stand at the room's other door, poised to leave.

"I knew you were eavesdropping," she says evenly. "Add 'no privacy' to my list." She slams the door.

I listen. I can hear drawers being yanked out. The sliding sound of a suitcase, I guess, being pulled from beneath the bed. It all sounds serious.

Eavesdropping is an unfair accusation. When the words are so loud they pound your ears, you're not trying to listen in; you're trapped into hearing. There's a big difference. And hearing things you know you have no right to be part of. But they're there. Unavoidable.

There are no words now. Just sounds. I think of Louie, lying there in bed, watching helplessly as Louray flings herself around the room gathering up her clothes. Next, she'll come into Honey's and my room, yanking out Honey's dresser drawers to snatch up her clothes, too. *Not with me here,* I think, and leave.

I am on the front porch when the taxicab comes. Louray points to the three suitcases just inside the front door, and the driver takes all three at once. No words are even spoken. I figure Louray has used up all her words. There aren't any left.

I know somehow I am at the heart of it all. What I don't know is that Louie thinks it is all his fault and Grandmorgan somehow feels it falls to her.

Grandmorgan and I watch them leave. Honey waves out the window until Louray snatches her arm down.

And now I begin my first day without Honey. Since she came home from the hospital where she was born, she's slept in my room except for that short time when Louie was off at watch school. Part of going to sleep is listening for her even breathing.

Honey being beside me somehow nails me to the planet. I wonder if I'll even be able to get to sleep without her there. Grandmorgan and I go back inside the house and silence sets in for days.

To escape the quiet, I go outside and mow our small front yard with the push mower. Smell the hot cut grass and let June heat me deep inside where hurtful times try to be cold.

Like the rest of the houses on the south side of Clay Street with large porches all across the front, Grandmorgan's house sits higher than the street, on a rise. The rise makes yards with steep banks, hard to mow. It's toward the end of that first week of Louray and Honey's being gone when the mowing is finally done, the dandelions have been dug up, and I'm cutting the edge grass at the curb with a pair of scissors, careful to avoid the area where Mr. Hadley's mule and wagon stand. I hear a voice calling.

"Hey, you! Hey, you, girl!"

I shade my eyes to look across the street where the voice is coming from. It's the boy who waved the day he moved in. We hadn't seen any of that family since that day. Their car had been gone for over a week, but, even when it was parked back out front, not one member of the family ever came out. Today, though, the boy is standing at his curb, his hands propped where hip pockets belong, elbows sticking back and out like bent wings.

"Hi," I call back.

"What are you doing?"

Well, I'm not cutting cloth, I think to myself. "What's it look like?"

He grins. "It looks just like you're cutting grass with a pair of scissors."

"I am."

He looks down the street toward Boulevard Drive, then back to me. "You cut your whole yard with scissors?"

"No." Surely just once he had looked out a window to see me fighting the lawn mower.

"Be mighty slow." He nods, to agree with himself. "Slow."

It is already the strangest conversation I've had in a long while, when he sews up the strangeness with the next question. Sews it up and double knots it. "Are you Dale Evans?"

I don't answer, it takes me back so.

"Because, if you are," here he pulls one earlobe then goes back to bracing his back with both hands, "you need to unhitch your horse there and put it on in the barn." The last part he says sort of soft, gentle. Like he's giving me good advice but doesn't want to offend.

"You're kidding," I say, praying he is but suspecting he might not be.

"No."

I watch to see if he'll crack up and, after a good

33

laugh, he'll say something that makes sense like, *Hi, I'm Don Woods and this coming fall I'll be going to your high school there at the end of the street.* He's old enough for high school at least.

I wait. When he doesn't crack, I think I'll just play along. "What gives you the right to tell me what to do with my horse?" I ask, motioning with my head toward Mr. Hadley's mule.

"Because I'm Roy Rogers," he says with a little swagger of his head.

"Right."

"And I'm an expert on horses."

"Well, for your information, Roy," I say, laying the scissors on the curb and crossing the street to stand nearer so we don't have to shout this weird conversation, "that there is a mule, not a horse. And I'm not Dale. I'm Shanta. And that mule belongs to Mr. Hadley, not me."

"Who's Mr. Hadley?"

His eyes are really serious. And very blue. I don't care if they're so blue they're purple, he's really taking this to an extreme.

"Do you always talk in code?" I ask, not wanting to embarrass myself by being so serious that the moment he shifts to reality I'll be left out on a limb somewhere.

"This isn't code. Who's Mr. Hadley?"

"He gardens my grandmother's side and back

plot. Lives in Kirkwood and drives his mule to get here."

"Why does he do that?"

I start to say, "You sure do ask a lot of questions," but, instead, I shrug and say, "Maybe he doesn't have space for a garden. I don't know." For me, Mr. Hadley gardening my grandmother's side yard is just natural, has been going on forever. I've always looked out the kitchen window in the spring and summer to see his farmer's straw hat bent between a row, shading him from the searing sun.

"Well, he definitely needs to water his horse and put him in the corral. Definitely."

He looks back up at the traffic on Boulevard Drive and I can't help noticing that he really is normal looking except that at one corner of his mouth a drool of spittle moistens a line from there down his chin. He licks at it from time to time.

If he'd just take his hands down, I'm thinking, when the screech of a screen-door hinge makes us both look to where one of his sisters, I guess, is coming across the yard toward us.

"Hey," the girl calls out, and I wonder if the horse dialogue is to continue.

"Is that *hey* as in *hi* or *hay* as for horse food?"

"What?" The girl walks over to us.

"Roy here, and I were just talking about horses," I say, feeling like an idiot. Parents can name their kids what they will, and we're stuck with the names. Look at me. Who wants a name like Shanta Cola? Maybe he really is named Roy Rogers. How do I know?

"Roy?" the girl asks, puzzled.

He looks over at her. "I *am* Roy Rogers. That *is* my name." He is reminding his sister, that simple. And he is so emphatic the spit flies.

She smiles. "Oh, my . . . golly!" Closing her eyes, she swallows hard, then takes a breath and begins. "This is Earl Walling. That's his real name. When we are pla—"

"NO, I'M NOT EARL!" he explodes. "I'm Roy—"

"Okay. Okay. Let's see . . ."

"Definitely not Earl. Definitely Roy." The tension is obvious as he prompts her.

The girl looks at the sidewalk when she asks me my name.

"Shanta. Shanta Cola Morgan."

That gets her full attention. "What a name," she whispers.

"Well, it's all mine," I say. "Odd, but all mine."

Then we sit down on the curb, the three of us, and I tell them why my parents chose my name.

"When they brought me home from Georgia Baptist Hospital, they brought me to an apartment on Briar Cliff Road, right across from Asa Candler's estate."

Earl takes in every word, but the girl stops me with a question.

"Who's Asa Candler?" She has a slight lisp when she talks, softening *c*'s and *s*'s, making them stand apart from the rest of the word.

"He's the Coca Cola Baron and is richer than God."

"Wow." The girl lets out a breath. "Were your parents rich, too?"

"Naw. They were just renting an apartment and I don't remember any of this but Grandmorgan and her friend Mrs. Findley drove me by there once when we went to the Krystal Hamburger place for lunch and they told me. Pointed it out to me."

"So . . . what's that got to do with your name?" the girl asks.

Earl punches and shushes her at the same time. "You let her be, Dennie. She's trying to tell us."

"I'm not sure why the *Shanta* part. They're dead now and I can't ask so I'll never know. But the middle name, *Cola,* is because of where we lived."

We all sit in silence, thinking about my strange name. Finally Earl's sister speaks up.

"I once knew a girl who was born on the Fourth of July and her mama named her 'Liberty Belle.'"

"Huh-uh," Earl sings.

"Yes, she did, Earl Thomas Walling. You just shut up! Go inside. I can't even talk with a friend without you butting your big head in—"

She stops cold because Earl is looking at her so steady with eyes that have already begun to brim with tears. They just look at each other and finally Dennie whispers, "Sorry, Earl," and rubs his arm.

I don't know what to say so I start up with my family again. "You want to hear a really funny name?"

They both nod.

"My Uncle Louie's name isn't *Louie* at all. It's Nym Hurt Morgan."

"Nym Hurt," they both say in unison.

"Yep."

"That's the ugliest name I've ever heard," Earl says, thoroughly awed. "What's your daddy's name?"

I tell them my parents were killed in an automobile accident and I had lived with my uncle and grandmother ever since. This is never easy for me to tell. It sets me apart. Makes me different because families always have a mother and a daddy. Or at least one of them. But I just go ahead and tell it to get it out of the way. I feel just like the Atlanta Crackers must feel. Grateful to be on any team but aching to play in the majors. I want more than anything to be in a real family. Had thought, with Louray coming, it was fixed. But now that she's gone, I'm back to Louie and Grandmorgan.

"Is she old?" Earl blurts. Evidently his hurt feelings don't last long because he asks the question like the world turns on my answer. "Your grandmother. Is she old?"

"Yeah. Pretty much."

"My mother's not old," he says with authority.

"Earl," the girl begins, then quickly corrects herself before his outrage has time to bloom, "Roy is different." He nods, and, since that is an understatement, definitely, as Roy would say, I just sit and say nothing in response. "He has a steel plate in his head." He obligingly shows me the scar. "He's twenty-one but has the mind of a five-year-old." He nods and smiles proudly.

Since that, too, is hard to comment on, I let a minute pass. It's probably not easy for the girl to tell this, like it is always awkward for me explaining my odd family. Finally I say, "Your name's Dennie?" The girl nods. "What's it stand for? Dennie."

"Short for Denise."

I haven't had a raft of friends because I never feel comfortable asking people home from school. Actually live in mortal fear somebody from school might show up some day and I'd have to ask them in and there would be my grandmother, older than God, and Uncle Louie, now flat on his back in bed. Getting acquainted is not a breeze. Not my strong suit. I am ashamed that I am ashamed, but I am. I just smile at Dennie and sit.

"My two sisters are Elizabeth," Dennie tells me. "She's fifteen, and Earnestine is seventeen. I'm twelve."

"She's twelve." Roy nods at me.

"I just turned thirteen in April," I tell her.

The screen door screeches again, and their mother steps out the front porch door to shake a rag rug. She looks at us as we turn to watch, doesn't speak, not even smile. I guess shaking the rug is serious business, she does it so long and hard. Then she turns and goes back inside.

"Who lives there?" Dennie asks, pointing to Mrs. Piersey's house next door.

I tell them about Mrs. Piersey and her son Jimmy away at war. "She hasn't come out of that house since the day he left."

"Why not?" Earl wants to know.

I shrug. "Maybe she thinks it's keeping him alive if she stays shut up inside. That's what we all think. Who knows? Neighbors visit her and friends. Bring her groceries. Maybe she feels like, if she went outside, she'd have a gold star to replace the blue one in her window within a week."

"A gold star?" Dennie asks.

"Means somebody at your house died in the war."

"Oh."

Then, I tell them about all the rest of the neighbors, while I'm at it.

"On my side, second house down toward Boulevard Drive, Preacher Weathers and his family lives. His son, second son, Ralph Edward, he's the meanest boy that ever lived. Steer clear of him."

Earl frowns and hates Ralph Edward sight unseen.

"Ever since we were little he's tried to bully me. They used to have a huge German shepherd named Butch. I was skating on the sidewalk once when I was about six years old and, as I passed his house, Ralph Edward turned Butch out into the yard and yelled, 'Sic 'em!' "

Earl's eyes are horror stricken. I guess he might be afraid of dogs and this story brings untold terror.

"You want me to stop?" I ask him.

He shakes his head so I continue. "Well, Butch sprang out of their yard, snarling and woofing for all he was worth."

I stop to swallow and Dennie asks, "What'd you do? Run?"

"No. Louie told me never to run if Butch ever got after me. He'd try to bite me if I ran. Anyway I was on skates so I would have had to skate away. I just froze and Butch circled me.

"I could hear Ralph Edward up on his front porch hissing, 'Sic 'em, Butch. Sic 'em!'

"I stayed right there on that spot on the sidewalk. Then Rowena Stewart, next door to us, came out to see what all the barking was about.

41

"'Here! You get away from her!' she started yelling at Butch, which just made him madder. He growled and eyed me with his evil eye and I almost wet my step-ins. Finally, Rowena went and got Grandmorgan. I watched her come off our porch, holding a broom.

"'Come on, Shanta!' she yelled. 'He's not going to hurt you.'

"I guess she didn't want to have to walk all the way to where I was to get me. But I didn't budge. I couldn't even raise my voice to answer. Much less my legs. Pigeons could have landed on me, I was so still."

"Did he bite you?" Earl asks.

I shake my head. "Nope. But finally Grandmorgan saw she was going to have to come get me. When she passed Rowena's hedge, I heard Ralph Edward's front screen door slam and knew he'd gone on back inside so he couldn't be blamed for anything.

"'Scram, dog!' Grandmorgan said in her I-mean-business voice, but I guess Butch didn't read her well. He turned on Grandmorgan and did his low-growl-mean-look act on the wrong person. Grandmorgan turned that broom around so fast she looked like a majorette at the head of a band in a football stadium at half time. Then she beaned the blooming heck out of that dog. I was sorry Ralph Edward wasn't there to see up close."

Dennie and Earl shout with laughter and I keep going.

"Butch's eyes crossed and he sort of weaved for a second. Then, when his senses returned, he howled like he'd pure near been killed, and tucked his tail, and flew up the bank to Ralph Edward's porch. When he got to the porch stairs, he turned back around and growled again.

"Grandmorgan took one step in his direction and shouted, 'You do it! You just come do it! I'll lay you out in the middle of the road in one blue minute!'

"She waved the broom and Butch yelped like a car had just broadsided him, smushed him to a ribbon. The front screen door mysteriously opened a foot or so and he went scrambling into the house. My theory is that Ralph Edward had crawled on his belly across the floor so he could open the screen without anybody seeing him. It was probably a good thing that he opened the door when he did because if my grandmother had cleared her throat good that dog would have punched in the screen on his way through."

"What'd your grandmother do then?" Earl wants to know.

"She just said, 'Come on home, Shanta,' and I skated along behind her.

"Man!" Earl breathes. "Is that dog still there?" He stands up and shades his eyes to see the very house Butch called home. Maybe even turns ever so slightly in case I say yes, so he'll be a jump ahead toward his own front door.

But I shake my head. "Nope. He attacked the postman a couple of years ago and they had to have him put to sleep." Then I add, "Not the postman. The dog," and the three of us laugh again and Earl sits down.

It gives me a feeling of power to have this much influence so I keep rolling.

"Right next door to us live two unmarried ladies, older ladies. Lelia and Rowena Stewart. They mostly clean their house, work in their yard, and chew gum."

Dennie brays out a laugh.

"It's true," I tell her. "Miss Rowena gets out there and waters the lawn. I think she times it by chews. She'll water the petunia pots for twenty chews, then move her hose to target the trellis area for about fifteen chews."

Earl loves this. He slaps his thigh several times and laughs loud.

"And Miss Lelia, she's courting."

"Courting?" he asks.

"Yep. She has a boyfriend who shows up every Thursday and Saturday night like clockwork. They sit in the front porch swing for hours."

"Doing what?" Dennie asks.

I shrug. "Just talking, I reckon."

"Who lives there?" Earl asks, pointing to McGolphin's house on the other side of ours.

"Well, my grandmother calls him the finest neighbor anybody could ever have. If you ever have trouble, he's the one to go to for help. He's old as Methuselah, but strong and acts rough. Underneath he's not mean, though. Just sounds that way."

"What about his mother?" Earl asks.

"He means his wife," Dennie says.

"His wife. What about her?"

"She's dead I guess." I shake my head. "As long as I've lived here she's never been there."

Next there is Mrs. Soap-Opera Paige on down past McGolphin. "Grandmorgan says she bellyaches about everything. And right there, beside your house, Mr. and Mrs. Warnock live. Her name's funny. Her first name is Tennis, like the game. They're nice. And I don't know people farther down the street."

When I finish, Dennie asks, "Does your granddaddy live with you?"

"No. I never knew him. Been dead for years."

"Then who brings home the money?" Earl asks.

I smile. "There's not much. It's a funny thing. Everybody else worries about ration books. At our house, that doesn't even come up. We've got enough ration stamps. We just don't have much money. My Uncle Louie fixes watches. Well, used to. He's taken to his bed now for about a month."

"There's a big clock in your yard," Earl points out.

"I know."

Grandmorgan calls me to come feed Louie his dinner. "I'll see you later, maybe," I tell them.

After I collect my scissors from the curb, I cross our yard to the clock sign. It doesn't take much tugging to work the metal legs out of the ground. Leaning it against the foundation of the house behind the althea bushes, I tell it, "I guess we won't be needing you for a while."

The watch customers have almost all come to collect their unfixed timepieces anyway.

4

Feeding Louie dinner is something I suddenly am counted on to do seven nights a week. Grandmorgan feeds him breakfast and lunch, but she needs a break. Dinner is mine. His food has to be soft and easy to swallow because he's lost most of his teeth. That, combined with lying on his back in bed, makes food hard to swallow. I have never had nerve enough to ask why his teeth had to be pulled and nobody volunteers a reason. At first Grandmorgan buys jars of Gerber baby food so he doesn't have to worry about chewing with only gums.

"What'd you eat for breakfast?" I ask him this night as I feed him. It's really just making conversation because time passes faster when we talk.

"Scrambled yeggs and grits." Louie always calls eggs "yeggs," just for the fun of it, I guess.

"Lunch?" I pop a spoonful of pureed green beans into his mouth. The little jars stand in a pan of hot water so they'll be more "palatable," Grandmorgan calls it.

"Cream of Wheat."

I want to say, "Yuck!" Eating Cream of Wheat ranks up there with choking down cooked carrots, but you don't want to knock the only thing a person can eat.

In the quiet times I can hear the little fake duck on Louie's mantel bobbing up and down to the water in a cup in front of it. It squeaks each time it comes back up, ticking away the mealtime the way a clock would time.

"Who gave you that duck?" I ask, looking across at it.

"Harold Hendrix."

We watch together.

"Are the beans good?" I ask as I feed him a spoonful.

"*Así, así,*" he says.

I look up. "What's that mean?"

"Oh," Louie says. "*Lo siento.*"

"Huh?"

"That means 'I'm sorry' in Spanish."

"What does the *así, así* mean?"

" 'So-so.' "

"Where'd you learn that?"

He reaches to a shelf under his bedside table and pulls out a Spanish textbook. "Beginning Spanish," he reads aloud.

I set the spoon down and open the book. On the first page I see a drawing of the sun rising. Reading aloud, I say, "*Buenos días.*"

"Good for you," Louie says. "*¿Cómo estás?*"

"Ha! I found it, 'Fine thanks' . . . oh! Wait! *Bien, gracias.*"

Louie grins and motions to the food getting cold. I lay the book on the bed beside him and feed him more.

"How long you been studying Spanish?" I ask.

"*Cuatro* days," he says, holding up four fingers. Then he holds his hand up to stop me. "*La cortesía mucho vale y poco cuesta.*"

I blink. Have no idea. "I give."

"Look on page one."

I pick the book back up and open it to page one. "Oh, at the bottom . . . 'Politeness is worth a lot and costs little.' Huh."

I resume feeding him and think how Louie had said that just in the nick of time. Turning the page with my left hand, I think how he might have chosen the saying on page two. It is, "A bird in the hand is worth two in the bush." I am glad he chose the one on politeness because I had been on the brink of asking if he was planning a trip to Spain or Mexico. Now I realize that would be impolite. Instead I ask, "Where did you get the book?"

"Harold brought it when he visited the other night."

I close the book and feed him, each of us absorbed in our own thoughts. At one point Louie says, "You are feeding me *cena o comida*."

"That's a lot of words for 'beans.'"

"No. That means 'dinner.' I don't know 'beans' yet." We both laugh at his pun.

My mind begins to wander in the quiet. First, I think how I could tell Dennie and Earl about the Spanish. Maybe I can teach them. Then I think about Honey. How I won't be able to teach her Spanish. How I miss her in the big double bed at nights, talking after the light is turned out. Remember she was scared of the dark. Even though morning had come, she stayed under the pillow until she woke.

Wonder how she handles that now? I think.

Even though Honey's questions almost drove me wild at times, the memories rise that underscore her absence. I wonder how in the world Louie handles the quiet and the missing.

Of course, his magician friends that have started dropping in almost every evening now are helping to cheer him up. I'm sure they are. Harold Hendrix is always pulling eggs from my ears. In the winter. No eggs in the summer. I ask him why not.

"Because eggs might spoil in the heat," he had told me, and winked.

I know, though. No long shirt sleeves for him to hide the egg up. I know.

Mr. Julian isn't as easy to second guess. It's like dealing with God when you tangle with Mr. Julian. What he says is so loud.

"I'm not happy here, Shanta," he says when his iced tea glass sweats and drips on his trousers.

I get a crocheted coaster for him. Grandmorgan made two dozen of them.

"Not the right color," he booms, and I get green this time.

"Nope!"

Louie is grinning the whole time.

By the time I bring red then purple, I'm worn out and Mr. Julian agrees it's just the right color.

"Now put these all back," he says, pointing to the stack on his knee, while he slides the purple coaster onto his tea glass.

As I put them back in the sideboard drawer, they feel funny. Crisp. I take the top one back out and inside it is a new, flat, and smooth dollar bill. And so it is with the other four. When I look across the room, Mr. Julian frowns and puts his finger to his lips and says, "I kept telling you I wasn't happy with the color. So . . . sue me."

The magicians almost always visit early evening, but dinner time belongs just to Louie and me.

Sometimes, to make it move faster, Uncle Louie and I play a game called "I'm Hiding." I think it might be a good time to play it so I say, "In English . . . I'm hiding somewhere in this room."

Louie catches the spirit of the game at once and asks, "How small are you?"

"No taller than a thimble, but flatter."

He sucks water through a bent glass straw. "Behind the picture."

"Which one?" I ask, spooning in pureed prunes.

"The one of my high school graduating class."

I shake my head.

"The one beneath it."

I look. It is a picture of Louray and Honey in Grant Park. Louray is pushing Honey on a swing. I guess Louie had taken it. I look back at him, but he's still looking at the picture. And when he finally looks to me, his eyes are overflowing and he says he is through with dinner, though he's only eaten a third of it.

That night I am still having a hard time getting to sleep. Now I think about how much pain is bumping along one room over. But mentioning the pain or even Louray or Honey is somehow forbidden, though no one actually says it. It is one of those unspoken laws, like the fact of my feeding Louie dinner seven nights a week. I feel sure I am the reason Louray left but wouldn't bring it up if my life depended upon it.

Sometime during the night I am awakened by a loud noise. A crash. Splintering and urgent. But sleep has been so slow to come that I can't leave it once it is finally here so I lie still and listen.

"Mother," Louie calls. And again, "Mother!"

But Grandmorgan doesn't hear and, since my name hasn't come up, I lie still, folded at the edge of sleep.

"Shanta," I hear as I sink away, but not one part of me struggles against the sleep.

I awake the next morning to the sound of splintered shards being swept into a dustpan in Louie's room.

"Why didn't you call me?" Grandmorgan's stooped-over voice asks.

"I did," Louie replies. "But you couldn't hear."

It is only a glass pitcher of water Louie keeps so he doesn't have to bother anybody every time he needs a drink. Not crystal, just glass. Replaced easily enough by another in the kitchen cupboard. My gnawing guilt over not coming to his aid is much dearer than the pitcher. That guilt could be a polished diamond the way I stow it in the safekeeping of my mind and go to visit it every day after that, alongside the guilt already in place over Louray's leaving because she thought I was teaching Honey to cuss.

The next night McGolphin brings over an intercom system. When Louie holds down a button on a speaker box, he can tell Grandmorgan back in her bedroom next to the kitchen what he needs. And then she can tell him right back that he'll have to wait 'til she can get to it. Except she shouts it so loud people on Peachtree Street probably hear her.

"Just talk normal," McGolphin tells her. "Morgan, you're not trying to contact Generalissimo Chiang Kai-shek." But it does good only for the moment. Five minutes later she forgets and yells to Louie words that are so distorted you think she's speaking in a foreign tongue.

McGolphin grins at Louie. "Tell you what. We'll just have to help her remember," he says.

He goes home and gets some purple construction paper and makes a sign bigger than all get-out. Sticks it to Grandmorgan's speaker with adhesive tape. It says, *Talk normal!*

"That's not necessary, McGolphin," she tells him in a huff when he returns to sit with Louie.

"Oh yes 'tis, Morgan. And if that don't work, I can adjust the wiring so's hit gives a little buzz to your hand to remind you each time . . ."

"No, thank you!" She stalks out of Louie's room but not before she hears their laughter. Louie's and McGolphin's.

"I swear," McGolphin says, raring back in his chair, "I don't think I've ever seen anybody's mouth flop so wide as hers did that evening she touched the electric fan and the light switch at the same time." He pitches a high, wheezing laugh so tight he can't continue.

There'd been a short in the fan and Grandmorgan had about set a new world record for volume and high jump, simultaneously.

"You could see," Louie says for McGolphin, "that thing in the back of her throat . . ." Then he convulses, too, into laughter.

"Her diphthong," McGolphin cuts back in to say.

"Diphthong!" I burst out. "That's her uvula," I tell them, but it only sets them off again. "I learned that in health this year . . ." But Louie's laugh is high like McGolphin's and he says at that same pitch, "I liked diphthong better."

It occurs to me later that for the first time since Louray and Honey had left, there had been laughter in our house. First Spanish, now laughter. Maybe we're going to make it to the other side of this deep river after all.

Harold Hendrix helps set up with a home health nurse to come once a week to give Louie a bath so Grandmorgan isn't called upon to do that. Every Thursday night. Even the magicians learn that Thursday nights are sacred. And several of the magicians get together and buy Louie a hospital bed so a person doesn't have to lean down to bathe or feed him. He lies in that bed against one wall and when I'm not feeding him, sometimes I sit on the antique bed with the wooden clocks and visit.

Grandmorgan never once seems to think of herself as the recreational director of this house. Not when I arrived as a little girl, not when Louray and Honey lived there, and not now that Louie is bedridden. She keeps doing what she's always done with some adjustments.

It's a good thing that somebody has moved in across the street to take Honey's place. I would be a maniac without Dennie and Earl. It's gotten so I sit on our steps after breakfast every morning and wait until they finish their chores and can come out. Granted, Dennie and I might play less and talk more if Earl weren't around wanting to play Roy Rogers every living minute. But at least it's somebody besides my own household and it's outside in the sunshine. Our house is so big and hollow these days.

Sometimes, sitting out there on the front steps, I hear sounds from the Wallings' house. Mainly two voices. A high voice that tightens my insides just hearing it. I catch myself grimacing as Mrs. Walling's high, blurred words come across Clay Street.

But then the deeper voice takes over, pounding out words like he's printing newspapers. It's the same voice I heard tearing Earl up over the broken lamp on their moving day. A tall, lean printing press of a man, making black and white memories of June mornings on Clay Street behind the walls of his house.

But Dennie never refers to it. You'd think Blondie and Dagwood are her parents, she's so calm and glad to see me.

Once a month, Mrs. Findley, a lady friend of Grandmorgan's, comes over in her Packard and they drive with me in tow to Westview Cemetery to trim the graves. Since Louie took to his bed, I don't go with them, which suits me fine because all it had ever amounted to, for me, was cutting grass around the tombstones with scissors and putting flowers from Woolworth's in the metal urns. I would hear them talk, Grandmorgan and Mrs. Findley, about their dead husbands and how they missed them and on and on. Now that Louie is taken by arthritis, I stay behind to listen out if he needs anything.

This day, while Grandmorgan and Mrs. Findley are at Westview Cemetery, I am sitting on the antique bed visiting with Louie when the phone rings. I hop right up to get it. And there on the other end is Louray.

"Hi, Shanta," she says in her smooth voice.

"Hi."

"What are you up to?"

She sounds chipper. And she doesn't mention right off the bat that Honey is cursing like a drunken sailor. That's good. But Louray sounds too happy for somebody whose marriage is unraveling. It rankles me. Then I remember McGolphin laughing that night when he hitched up the intercom system and how it had made me feel. That we'd be making it with or without Louray. Louray needn't know Louie sobs some nights, and sometimes Grandmorgan and I mope around missing Honey. She doesn't need to know any of that.

"Well," I tell her, sounding all excited like life on Clay Street is throbbing, "Grandmorgan and Mrs. Findley have gone on their monthly trip, snipping and remembering at Westview Cemetery, and Louie's got company, and I'm getting ready to go across the street to play with the new neighbors. We're busy as bees."

I smile to think how wonderful our house sounds.

"Who's visiting Louie?" Louray asks.

"I don't know her name," I lie. There isn't anybody else in that room with Louie but that drinking duck bobbing away on the mantel.

"Well," Louray says, "tell him I called." The phone cord isn't near long enough to reach all the way to Louie's room. "Tell him I might come round to see him before too long and bring Honey."

I want to hit her it makes me so mad. MIGHT come! MIGHT bring Honey! But I hold on to my hat and say, "Okee dokey. 'Bye." And I hang up first. Anybody that would put somebody as wonderful as Louie through what Louray is putting him through deserves to be hung up on.

"Who that be?" Louie asks as I cross through his room.

"Louray." Then I tell him some of what Louray said. The part about she might come soon.

"I'm not holding my breath," he says quietly.

When Grandmorgan gets back, I tell her about the call, out of hearing of Louie, not wanting him to know I'd hung up on Louray.

"Good for you!" Grandmorgan bursts out. "I'm glad you did. She deserves to be hung up on. It'll be a cold day you-know-where when she ever comes calling. I'll be willing to wager on that!"

"Do you miss her?" I ask Grandmorgan, meaning Honey.

"Who? Louray? Not a bit in this world. What's to miss?"

"I mean Honey," I say.

She works her mouth into a knot. Twice. Before she answers.

"Jess," she says and that's all. It's as close as she'll ever come to saying how bad it hurts her.

Then Grandmorgan shows me a hat Mrs. Findley has given her. "Says she's tired of it. I don't know. What d'ya think?"

It's awful. It looks like a burnt pancake, stiff, with grapes glued on the side. We each try it on and look in the mirror to laugh.

The next day the hat finds a home. It is the first step in Grandmorgan's new campaign. Her campaign to help us all through a desperate time. A time when we are living so close to the bone that snacks are bread crusts sliced off of Grandmorgan's lunchtime sandwiches and saved in a bread wrapper. When hunger strikes, Grandmorgan and I go grab a few bread crusts and stave off the craving until mealtime. Crusts last a person a lot longer than Popsicles and cost less, though Grandmorgan still gives me change from time to time to buy one from the man who rides down our street with an ice chest attached to his motor scooter.

We are each handling the hard times in our own way. Louie has taken up Spanish. Somehow that seems to help. Keeps his mind occupied with something besides Louray and Honey. Now Grandmorgan is finding her own way through it.

"We need," Grandmorgan says this Thursday morning in late June, "to do something wacky every single day from now on till we're back on dry land." She plops the pancake hat back on her head and studies herself in the mirror.

Aha! She is seeing it as a river, wide and deep, same as I do, I think. "Wacky?" I ask out loud.

"There's a song goes 'Do-Wacky-do'," Grandmorgan says. "It means something . . . different from normal . . . taking a chance . . . crazy."

She won't play games with me or help me find somebody who will, but she has taken it upon herself to do something out of the ordinary so we don't all the time think about our problems. I don't know exactly what my tack will be, but I feel that something will pop up sooner or later, just when I need it most. And that will be how I survive in tough circumstances.

"Up in the attic," Grandmorgan continues as she goes into the kitchen to wash up Louie's breakfast dishes, "there's an old dress form."

"What's that?"

"It's a wire woman, is what it is." She flicks off the faucet and turns to me. "Bosoms and all. It's what I used to fit my dresses on when I sewed. Shanta, you and I are going up there and pass that form through the opening. Come on! Let's go before it heats up hotter than blue blazes."

I follow Grandmorgan up the stepladder she set up to reach the trapdoor in the hall ceiling, walk bent over near the edges, careful of rafters, and endure the heat I feel has already passed the blue blazes marker. I hold the flashlight while Grandmorgan locates the wire woman and watch as she rolls the dress form to the opening in the attic floor. Grandmorgan backs carefully and slowly down the ladder a few rungs.

"Here now, Shanta, lay your torch down and tip her on her side. Just lay her right down on the floor. That'a girl. Now slide her, rollers first, on into this hole, but hang on to her. I'll walk her down slow soon as I've got her good."

I do it all. Hold to the wire contraption as Grandmorgan slowly pulls it with her while she descends the ladder.

"Now," Grandmorgan says, shutting the sliding trap door with the soft end of a dust mop, same as she had opened it.

Wheeling the dress form into her bedroom, Grandmorgan stares at it. I sit down with a grunt. Turning that wire woman into something that needs to be on this floor of the house instead of up in the attic is going to take more magic than my grandmother possesses. I am convinced of it.

"Can I go across the street and play with Dennie?" I ask.

Grandmorgan looks over at me. "You don't think I can do it, do you?"

"Do what?"

"Turn this contraption into a woman."

I look at the torso of metal bars forming a sort of cage and shake my head. "Nope," I answer and leave for Dennie's house. As I cross the street, I see Mrs. Piersey ironing just inside her open front door. *Getting fresh air,* I think. I wish Mrs. Piersey would look up so I can at least wave to her. I feel sorry the old lady is a prisoner in her own home. But Mrs. Piersey keeps nose to the grindstone and deals with a pillowcase like the King of England will be sleeping on it. Or Winston Churchill, one.

Before I can knock on the Wallings' front door, I hear Mrs. Walling's steel-cold voice doing her solo, resounding through the house and out the front door.

If sound had color, I think as I stand there — an uneasy listener — *her voice would be blue, deep ocean blue and gray. Even when she's not mad it's cold and shuts people away from her.*

I don't know whether or not to knock. I should have waited on my steps like normal, but wanting to tell Dennie and Earl about the wire woman got the best of me. I'm deciding whether to stay or leave. I just stand.

". . . because," Mrs. Walling drones far off in another room, "it takes my time and yours to go over it twice. When you dust take your cloth and go down the legs of the chair and while you're bent over, go ahead and do the horizontal rungs, too. Do you understand?"

I can't hear whoever answers her. *What a horrible way to spend a summer morning,* I think, *learning to be a perfect duster. You'd thing she was cleaning the White House.*

Earnestine crosses the living room and looks up to see me standing at the screen. "What d'ya want?"

she asks curtly. "Dennie's with mother and can't play."

Earnestine, as the oldest, is also the prettiest of the three girls. Dennie looks most like her. They both have hair so dark brown it's nearly black and eyes to match. Earnestine has gotten her figure, being seventeen, and has long, tanned legs. I envy her those legs and her figure. But Earnestine has lost pleasantness and joy along the way. *No wonder,* I think this morning. It's amazing to me that Dennie still has all of that inside her somehow.

I start to speak and find I'm hoarse. Clear my throat and try again. "Earl?"

"I'll see if Earl's finished his chores and can come out." She sounds like a teacher, jumping to make my one word fragment into a question.

Definitely you can't come in here. That's what's implied. Wonder what we'll do when winter hits? I turn to look at our house across the street. See the *29* nailed to the front porch upright. Notice the sagging front porch screens. That isn't high on our list right now. Eating followed closely by avoiding going naked are much more urgent matters. Last year's clothes are already too small for me and where will new clothes come from? I can't wear screening. I know this much.

I hear Earl coming and turn to see him as he walks purposefully to the door. Earl never ambles. It isn't in him. He moves with a directness just to get it over with and reach his destination.

"Wanna play?" I ask.

"Sure."

"Wanna play Roy Rogers?" Do the Georgia Crackers play baseball? Does Hershey make chocolate bars? Wrigley, gum?

"Yep."

"Roy, could we vary this a little? Like maybe you be the Cisco Kid and . . ."

"Uh-huh!"

"How about the Lone Ranger . . . or Hopalong Cassidy?"

He crosses his arms and glares through the screen at me.

"Okay, okay. You be Roy Rogers and I'll be Gorgeous George."

He eyes me suspiciously. "Who is Gorgeous George?"

"He's a professional wrestler. He has blond curls and golden bobby pins to hold them in place. It can be Roy Rogers meets Gorgeous George and they ride the range together."

"Are there bad guys?"

I huff in frustration. "Of course there are bad guys. Nothing happens if there aren't any bad guys."

Earl ponders all of this. New scenarios are not comfortable for him.

"Come on . . . Roy," I encourage him. "Learn to step out, do something different." But he hangs back.

I fear that he might not be allowed outside if he lingers long enough for Mrs. Walling to finish her lesson on dusting furniture with Dennie. She might start on Earl next.

"But, where's Dale Evans and you're a girl," he says. "You can't be Gorgeous George. He's a guy."

"I'll explain it when you come out." Who would believe you'd carry on this conversation with a person twenty-one years old. I turn, crossing the porch and trip down the stairs in double time. It wears me out to wrangle with Earl. Maybe it isn't worth it. Maybe I'll just go back and help Grandmorgan with the wire woman.

But he comes. Like a bull charging across an open field. Mad that I walked away. He kicks a wagon Dennie has left at the side of their walk. He is just past the wagon when it begins to roll on its own. It picks up speed and Earl glances back to see it coming across the yard. It passes him and rolls faster, bumping onto the sidewalk. Earl begins running to catch it as it rolls down by the Warnocks' house. Faster. Earl gallops as fast as his legs will carry him. I watch in amazement. Earl finally passes the wagon.

"Yeah!" I cheer.

But no. When he turns around and sees it heading squarely for him, he whips back around and takes

66

off at the speed of light. Like a Bengal tiger is in hot pursuit, Earl bellows in terror, his arms pumping at his chest hell-bent-for-election. He streaks up that hill, burning up the sidewalk.

At the bottom of the hill, when the sidewalk bends up in front of it, the wagon slows and finally stops and rolls backward into the grass. But Earl is halfway up the hill before he realizes he is safe.

Meanwhile, I have collapsed in the yard and am laughing so hard I can't breathe. Earl storms back to the wagon, yanking it around and bringing it on up to his yard.

Next he pounds over to where I am sprawled laughing beneath the oak tree that takes up most of the yard to the right of the front walk.

"I'm here," he announces, pouncing on the *here* so hard it sounds like a response to a roll call. "And what's so funny?" His eyes are angry slits and he is breathing heavy from the sprint and the anger as he sits on the ground.

"You," I say without hesitation and sit up. "Oh, Earl, you are wonderful! I love you, Earl Walling," and I fall backwards again in hysterics.

He blinks and takes that in. A smile, small, begins at the corners of his mouth and gradually blooms. When it fills his whole face, he looks over at me.

"I love you, too, Shanta."

It stops me cold because I have meant one thing and he has meant another. I sit up and look over at

Earl. Instantly I know he has just given me something he has never given anyone else before.

"Shanta," he says, spitting such a volume that I am glad we are three feet from each other, "would you be my girlfriend?"

Whoa! I'm not getting myself into this. I've started it and it's my fault. But no way. Being girlfriend could bring on nine thousand obligations here. For instance, I might have to come over or call daily.

"I like to know I can skip days coming over. I don't want to *have* to come," I tell him gently and add, "Earl." My hand reaches across and pats his. It's sort of the truth and sort of not. I can't bring myself to say I don't want to be the girlfriend of a guy who plays Roy Rogers all day.

He doesn't move his hand, but his smile closes up. "Then you won't?"

I shake my head. "No, Earl."

He thinks about that. "But you could be my girlfriend AND not come every day."

"What would your girlfriend have to do?"

He smiles again. There is hope after all.

"Well . . ." He holds up a finger for each chore he ticks off. "She'd have to hold my hand. Kiss me. And tell everybody she's my girl."

"Nothing doing. I'm not into kissing. No, Earl."

"Roy." It hasn't taken him the blink of an eye. I have stepped on Earl so he'll leave. Roy, strong

68

and confident, is needed to take over here. "Roy Rogers."

And definitely not tied to Roy Rogers, I think. "I'll be your friend."

He stares coldly across the street at my house. "For life."

He doesn't budge.

"Well, that's the best I can offer," I say.

We sit that way a few minutes. Finally Earl glances over at me. "Well, are we going to play or not?"

"Okay," I say. "You be Roy Rogers and I'll be Gorgeous George."

"Who's Gorgeous George?"

And, with the question, I know his memory won't hold the hurt he is feeling for long either.

When time for lunch comes, I leave to go home. As I pass Uncle Louie's door I see they are visiting with a lady as Grandmorgan feeds him his lunch. I go back to the kitchen and put together a peanut butter and honey sandwich. I wash it down with milk and head on back up front to go to Dennie's. The lady is still visiting up a storm.

"I'm going back over to the Wallings'," I lean in the doorway to say.

"Shanta," Grandmorgan calls, beckoning with her hand to waylay me, "come here a minute. There's somebody I want you to meet."

I come on into the room.

"Betsy, this here is my granddaughter, Shanta Cola Morgan. Shanta, this is Miss Betsy Manikin."

First off, I notice this woman is wearing the hat Mrs. Findley gave Grandmorgan. A veil that hadn't been on the hat before is pulled down over her face almost to her chin. She has on a long sleeved house-dress, stretching to the floor, and an apron.

"Reach here in Miss Betsy's pocket, Shanta," Grandmorgan says.

"I'd rather lift her veil and look at her face," I answer, leaning in that direction.

"Not!" Grandmorgan smacks my hand. "You leave her face be. I did the best I could now."

Really she has done a remarkable job. Except for being stiff, it actually does look like a person because the veil hides all the shortcomings and the fact that her sleeves are empty doesn't strike you at first glance because they are long.

"Can't I just see how you fixed her face?"

"Oh, all right. I just took a used oatmeal box and stuck a face on it."

She has. The pale pink paper she has covered the box with looks like her own rosy skin and she has given the manikin a three-dimensional look by jutting out a nose and eyelashes. Of course, she doesn't have a chin, but then some people don't.

"Reach in her apron pocket," Grandmorgan insists.

70

I do and pull out a piece of Super bubble gum. "Where'd you get this? You can't even buy it anymore. I thought they'd stopped making it because of the war."

"They may have," Grandmorgan tells me. "I put some back to give to the magicians' kids and then I forgot about it. You'd better be careful now. It might pull your teeth plumb out it's so old."

That night, when the magicians come calling, no kids are with them so I swipe three pieces of bubble gum and carry them across the street for Dennie and Earl and me. Mrs. Walling is sitting on their front porch, drinking beer and watching the comings and goings at our house.

"Who are all those men visiting your house?" she asks me after a swig of beer. "Mighty busy place."

These are the first words she's ever spoken to me. I've never seen Dennie's daddy after that first day and, to be honest, don't really know if her mother knows my name.

I think about it. It's none of her business really, but I don't want to be rude. No, actually I don't care about being rude. The question is rude. I just don't want to suffer the consequences . . . not seeing Dennie and Earl. So I open my mouth to answer when she jumps in to say, "If I didn't know better, I'd say your grandmother was running a house."

Then she laughs a chipping laugh. Sounds like a puppy yapping.

I don't smile. Actually I'm not sure what she means. *A boarding house?* I wonder.

But then my mind opens up. I think I know. She means the kind of house Belle Wattling ran in *Gone With the Wind.* She means a whore house. So I say, "They're friends."

"We got friends, too," she wheezes, then has a coughing fit. "But they don't come every night."

Dennie gets up from where she's sitting on the front steps. She turns and goes up onto the porch, and in a very even voice she says what she says, but I hear the steam underneath. I figure if her mother gets smart with Dennie at this point, Dennie will blow into fourteen pieces and won't even think about the consequences.

"Mom, you do have friends. Shanta's uncle can't get out to see his friends like you can yours. He's bedridden. So they come to see him."

She turns and comes out the porch door and down the steps, doesn't stop until she's crossed the street and is sitting on the curb in front of Miss Lelia Stewart's house. Like she's chosen sides.

Mrs. Walling doesn't so much as let a peep. At least not until Earl and I are out of earshot across the street with Dennie. Then if she says anything we don't have to hear it.

5

One morning in early July I hear on the radio news that America is threatening Japan to either give up or face total destruction, whatever that means. Our lives at 29 Clay Street, South East, are so tight it's hard to keep my mind on the war. We are up against so much, ourselves.

Almost every night after I go to bed, over the sound of Louie's radio with a late baseball game going full steam, I can hear him crying softly in the next room, hurting for Honey . . . even Louray, I guess. And, though Grandmorgan doesn't cry where I can see or hear her, she does do a lot of out-loud praying. Morning, noon, and night. She is also canning vegetables for winter. The buying of

73

baby food at the grocery lasted only about two weeks. Until the food money ran out. Then Grandmorgan started mashing up fresh vegetables from the garden. What little money Louie had brought in from fixing watches and Louray contributed had been enough to get by on. Now that those few dollars are gone, we are in dire straits.

Once a month Grandmorgan receives a check from social security for my dead grandpa I never saw. *Funny,* I think, *how a person you never knew is still right here helping out even after he's gone.* And I thanked that dead grandpa every time the envelope with the check in it showed up.

Now, as if the sudden shortage of money isn't enough, here Louray shows up on the first Saturday in July, and, this is funny it's so impossible, she wants Louie to pay her child support for Honey. Oh, and she doesn't bring Honey with her. Now, to me, that's cruel. What she did is mean enough, leaving Louie, and for all I know he might be so mad he never wants to see her again. But he has to want to see Honey. We all do. But, no. Louray knocks on the screen door about eleven o'clock this Saturday morning, and, when I dart to the door to see who's there, Louray whispers, "Let me in, Shanta, but don't tell Louie. I want to surprise him."

I let her in and leave. Go across the street. Can't bear to be part of whatever Louray has in mind.

"Aren't you curious why she's here?" Dennie asks as we sit on her front steps.

"It's not I don't care what she's come to say," I tell her and the listening but uncomprehending Earl. "It's surely not that she's coming back. I think maybe I care too much. It'd be like watching a killing. I can't. I just can't."

Dennie pats my arm, and, of course, Earl has to, also. No matter that he doesn't understand, at least he and Dennie care about me and the hurt I'm holding.

Earl is drawing pictures in a tablet with some crayons.

"What you drawing, Earl . . . Roy?" I ask him.

He holds the picture out so both of us can see. "Guess."

Dennie shoots me a quick look. She purses her lips, thinking hard. Finally she ventures a guess. "It's a long dinosaur with a mosquito on his back."

Earl lifts both legs off the ground and leans back to laugh hard. "No," he finally manages. "It's mother."

Dennie blinks and looks again. "What's she doing on the ground?"

Earl turns the drawing to himself to look again. "She's short."

"Not that short. And if that's not a mosquito on her back, what is it? A star?"

Earl frowns.

I feel sorry for him. "It's good, Roy." He looks up to see if he can trust me and I smile. "Really." He relaxes and returns my smile. "Can you draw your dad?"

Earl nods and goes at it with a passion.

Dennie and I watch my house to see when Louray will spill out into the scorching sunlight. The vegetable man rides slowly down Clay Street ringing his bell. No takers this hot morning, though.

"Here," Earl says and holds the next drawing for me to see.

"Wow," I whisper and take it from Earl. He feels wonderful.

"Now I'm drawing me," he sings.

I just look at the drawing. It fills the page. While the drawing of Earl's mother had been only at the bottom margin, this drawing of his daddy goes to all perimeters.

"Looks like a horse's face," Dennie whispers. "With horns. And it's unconscious because the eyes are *x*'s."

"I hear you, Dennie," Earl bellows like a baritone in an opera but doesn't slow down in his drawing. "Just you wait till you see *this* one." Finally he finishes with a flourish, and, putting the crayon beside the orange Crayola box, he holds up his picture. "Me," he says with great satisfaction.

"Oh, my golly," Dennie says, and Earl takes it as a supreme compliment.

I nod to show Earl how interested I am, but what I see is little more than chicken scratch. There is a *D* turned on its flat side with eyelashes coming beneath it. I know it is an eye, a closed eye. The left eye is an empty letter *P*. I guess a cupped line further down is the mouth. "A checkered vest?" I look up to ask when I notice the line down the middle of the page and boxes drawn in the bottom part.

Earl just smiles.

"Big checkers," Dennie says under her breath.

"Well, Roy," I tell him, "you really can draw."

He reaches for the tablet and flips to a fresh page. "Now I'll draw you," he says.

I wonder what I will look like coming off the end of Roy's crayon. Will I have eyes shaped like the letter *Q*, ears like basketballs, a mouth to rival the River Nile? I watch as Earl works at a feverish pitch. Then from deep inside Dennie's house I begin to hear an angry voice getting louder and more insistent as the minutes pass. I'm not exactly sure when my focus shifts from watching Earl and keeping an eye on my own front door through which Louray will surely explode or slink, depending on the success of her visit, to what is stirring deep inside the Wallings' house. I can't make out words but the angry burr of the voice is hard to ignore after a while. It is a man's voice. Probably their daddy. I've noticed both of the men are home during the day sometimes, and I figure they must work nights. I've never asked, though. If Dennie or Earl don't bring it up, neither will I.

Suddenly, another sound makes me lift my eyes to Dennie's. It is a scream.

Earl stands up fast, spilling crayons all down the steps. "Somebody's hurting Earnestine," he says urgently. "Somebody's slapping her."

"Sit down, Earl," Dennie orders and, for once, he doesn't protest the name.

No more screams come through their bulging front door screen. We all listen hard.

"What's wrong?" I get brave and finally ask Dennie because somehow Dennie seems to know.

"Earnestine didn't do the dishes right this morning. They're talking to her about it."

I just keep on sitting. I know that is a lie. Nobody gets this worked up over egg left on a plate. It has to be more than that.

But Dennie looks at me and says, "You'd better leave, Shanta."

And that is how I come to know that Louray is asking for money because I hear her as I come in our front door. And I hear Louie tell her there is none.

"Well, how do you expect Honey and me to live?" Louray asks.

What a question! Maybe she'll find a way to muddle through, I think, remembering the house where Louray lives — big, set well back from the street lined with such houses. We had gone there for lunch after their noon wedding.

I go for the back yard. Straight through the house and don't stop until I'm high in the mimosa tree. The whole world has gone crazy. People are demanding the impossible and not laughing like the joke it is. They are serious. The Pacific Ocean isn't the only battlefield. The one on Clay Street actually seems more hopeless, for the moment. Screaming over dirty dishes. Demanding money from empty pockets. A person should always have hope, even if it's only a small glimmer. I don't see much hope for us or Dennie's family.

That night the magician named Harold comes, back from a trip to Florida.

"Where it was hottern' hell," he tells Grandmorgan. "And I brought you something, Mrs. Morgan."

He pulls a tin of candy from a sack he's carried it in. "Do you like peanut brittle?"

"Well," she says, turning the orange can round and round in her hands, "if it's not too tough for my dentures to bite into."

"Try some," Harold encourages her. "Mavis and

I had some while we were sweltering in Ocala. It's crisp . . . surprisingly good."

He stretches out that word "surprisingly" and my salivary glands begin to work overtime. We always have an abundance of honey in the house because McGolphin keeps bees and he makes sure we never give out. But peanut brittle will be a treat.

"To be sure," Grandmorgan says, and I feel she is reading my mind about there being something different than honey to enjoy.

"Come over here, Shanta," Harold says and motions me over close to Louie's bed, I guess so I can have one of the first pieces.

Harold Hendrix wears frameless glasses that magnify his eyes to look like marbles. He watches Grandmorgan struggling with the lid but doesn't seem prone to pitch in and help her. Being independent, she is used to prying and banging to remove lids, so she works away on it.

Without any warning whatsoever, she pops the lid off and out of the open end of that can a long green coil, followed by a second, then a third, explode, reaching halfway into the living room when they stop bouncing and slithering. It is a silent explosion, but when those long, flying things shoot out of there Grandmorgan makes enough noise for seeing several snakes, and maybe a few other jungle animals, to boot.

"Whoo-whoo-whoo-whoo-whoo-o-oo!" rat-

tles out good and loud. She sounds like a south-
bound train approaching a crossing. I try to jump
right over top of Uncle Louie's bed, cowering as far
away from that can and its cloth snakes as I can get,
my ears ringing for five minutes from her yelling.

Harold takes his rimless glasses off he laughs so
hard. He and Louie deliver smacks to each other's
hands as they shout with laughter. Grandmorgan
holds on to her fifteenth *who-o-oo* the way the ca-
boose hangs on to the back of the train. When she
finally releases it, she practically flings her dentures
at the floor, she laughs so hard. It's wonderful. No
king in a castle, no president of the United States
of America ever had a better laugh. I don't think
we'll be able to stop, we're boiling away at it so.

Finally Harold gets his voice back. "Mrs. Morgan, I sure hope you'll forgive me for having a little
fun at your expense. You're a real good sport. You
know that?"

Grandmorgan smoothes out her housedress where
it has crawled a ways up her cotton stockings with
her foot stomping.

"Harold Hendrix, you beat all. I declare. Is it
mine to keep? The peanut brittle?"

"Yes, ma'am. Here, Shanta. Help me pick up
your grandmother's peanut brittle so I can dig in
my sack and find the real McCoy."

And the real McCoy, it is as hurting sweet as
those "snakes" are hurting funny. It lasts almost a

week. Well past the night Grandmorgan corners McGolphin sitting in there by Louie's bed. And under Miss Betsy Manikin's veiled gaze Grandmorgan offers McGolphin a piece of Harold Hendrix's peanut brittle.

"Now, don't you take no more'n two pieces, tops," she tells him, urging the can on him. "It's surprising how good it is." And she hangs on to "surprising" the way Harold had. I almost pop the elastic in my step-ins trying to hold back my laughing.

"No'm," McGolphin declines. "That stuff'll crack your teeth, Morgan."

"Not this. It's straight from Florida." And her mouth twitches a little, I reckon from the effort of restraining herself from grabbing McGolphin by the shoulders and shouting, "*OPEN THIS CAN, YOU OLD COOT!*"

Finally he sees she won't sit until at least he tries a bite.

"Just a mite then."

I think McGolphin's chair is going to turn right over, he jumps so high when those sudden snakes bolt past his popping eyes. And shout! He stops traffic downtown in front of Loewe's Grand Theater, he hollers so loud.

Well, Grandmorgan falls to laughing in fits. She'll almost be beyond it, then it will grab her again how funny McGolphin looked, clearing the air at least a foot over his head. Finally she reaches to the floor and hands him something.

"Here's your toothpick," she tells him. "Close your mouth around it. I've seen enough of your diphthong for one night."

McGolphin knows and so do we all, that is how she repaid him for teasing her before. But it's in good fun and it tickles him plenty that she counts she has gotten him back. As for Grandmorgan, she mutters and chuckles to herself off and on for days after.

Before I go to bed, Louie and I eat peanut brittle and listen to the Crackers win another game.

6

Peanut brittle isn't all that the magicians bring. Grandmorgan finds a folded five-dollar bill in Betsy's apron pocket one morning when she is replenishing it for the next onslaught of magicians' children. She takes it to the kitchen before she reacts.

"What's this?" she asks in a whisper as she unfolds the bill.

I come close to look over her shoulder. "Looks like a five-dollar bill," I say. "Where'd you get it?"

"Now don't you be telling Louie, you hear? I'm trying to piece this together. Let's see, last night Herb Hunter was over. Am I right?"

I nod yes.

"Well, how else is a five-dollar bill going to find its way into Betsy's pocket? Herb must have slipped it in after the children got their bubble gum out. I didn't see him, though."

And another day, she finds a ten, and it's a Friday morning. No one ever comes on Thursdays except the nurse, and she wouldn't have put money in the pocket. She doesn't even notice Betsy standing in her corner. That nurse is so busy scrubbing Louie down and talking about her grandchildren, it wouldn't be like her to do it.

"So it must have been from Wednesday night. Who came then?"

"Herb Hunter," I say.

"Well. I declare," Grandmorgan says in awe. "Can you beat that!"

And so it goes. Every so often Grandmorgan finds a little money in the apron pocket. She never tells Louie so he won't feel like it's charity. "It's a whole lot easier to accept a gift if you're not the one who's down and out. If you're only standing on the edges of that situation. And anyway, we'll count it as bubble-gum reimbursement money."

We both know it would buy a truckload of bubble gum, if it could be had. Thus I come to know that Grandmorgan never once feels down and out. She accepts the anonymous gifts as being given in love and never mentions them to a soul except me, and I tell no one either. Not even Dennie.

• • •

The hidden money is more practical, but the bombastic man named Mr. Julian brings Grandmorgan a gift she will never forget. It happens the night after he discovers Betsy Manikin.

"What's that standing there, Mrs. Morgan?" he asks, squinting at the manikin.

"It's Betsy," Grandmorgan answers back.

I watch as Mr. Julian lifts the hat veil. He is such a large, loud person, I never presume to call him "Julian," like I do Harold by his first name, or Herb Hunter by his. Mr. Julian looks at the oatmeal box face Grandmorgan has created. He rubs his chin, frowning a little.

Whirling around, he takes off his suit jacket and hangs it on the back of the chair he's been sitting in. Then he swings around to examine Betsy some more.

"You know," he says, a lot to himself, a little to Grandmorgan, and not at all to Louie or me, "I'll be willing to bet I could bring you a head. A real one."

He shifts to look at Grandmorgan, anxious that he hasn't offended her over the effort she has put into Betsy's face, nose and all.

But I'm the one who speaks. "A real head!" Mr. Julian is so powerful you're willing to believe almost anything he would come up with, but a *real* head?

My eyes look quick at Grandmorgan to see how she'd feel about having a real person's head in her house. As I look, my face begins to draw into a grimace over the thought of body parts coming into Louie's room. To stay. I know there are such things as shrunken heads. But here? In our house?

Mr. Julian catches my look. Stretching his neck up out of his tie-tight collar, he glances across at Grandmorgan.

"Yes, yes," he says thoughtfully. "You know, there's a gal at work who's been goofing off, drawing 'Kilroy Was Here' signs with lipstick on the bathroom walls and in general giving us all fits. I believe I could get her head for you by tomorrow night."

He walks over to stand beside Louie with his back to me. If I'd have looked closely I would have seen his shoulders shaking, but I'm too busy watching Grandmorgan.

"Where does he work?" I whisper furtively to her.

"Kesslers," Grandmorgan whispers back, straight-faced. "Kesslers Department Store. Down at Whitehall and Hunter. He owns it."

Mr. Julian takes a deep breath, loosens his tie, then turns with the air of a man who's come to a decision, rubbing his hands together, delighted that the plan is set. As he sits in his chair, he says straight to me, "I don't guess it matters that her name's 'Louise.' When we put her head on, she'll become 'Betsy.'"

I sit in silence. Don't know what to answer. In my heart I know, of course, Mr. Julian wouldn't be waltzing in with a real head on a platter, like Salome with John the Baptist's. But what the heck is he talking about? And he seems so positive about this head. So all-fired sure it will fit right on top of Betsy. I puzzle about it when I go to bed that night and off and on all the next day. That next night I hang around waiting for Mr. Julian to come, not willing to miss this for anything.

"Can you come over and play Kick-The-Can?" Dennie yells from the curb when I go out early evening to look for any cars turning onto Clay Street. "Elizabeth and Earl are going to play."

"I can't," I yell back. "Gotta help my grandmother," I lie.

Ralph Edward Weathers rides back and forth, up and down the middle of Clay Street on his bike, trying to show off. He's yet to make his move on me to get me back. But I'm wary all the same. I'll be ready. He's not a boy who'll forget being hosed down. The Wallings don't invite him into their game of Kick-The-Can, and I don't give him the time of day.

When Mr. Julian finally comes it's almost dark. He gets out on the driver's side, walks around the car, and, leaning inside, he then backs out with a large paper bag in his hands, shutting the door with a kick of his foot.

I scoot from the porch steps up onto the porch itself to open the door, then stand in the shadow of the swing as he strides past me and on into the house, holding the sack a good two feet in front of him.

"Hoo-hoo-hoo!" he bellows. "Anybody home?"

Louie calls, "*¡Buenos tardes!*" He is speaking more and more Spanish these days. "*¿Cómo estás?*"

"Well," Mr. Julian booms, "whatever you said, Louie. And back to you a hundredfold. I brought Louise."

It's more than I can stand. I have followed from the porch to the door of Louie's room, careful to stay on the safe side in case Mr. Julian is actually crazy enough to be bringing a real head, but close enough to watch. Now I go into the room, but still near the door.

Louie calls Grandmorgan on the intercom and she comes on the fly. When all has settled down, Mr. Julian reaches into the sack he has set on the chair on which he then hung his jacket. "Heeeer-r-r-re's Louise!" he calls.

Then he stops. Withdraws his hands and rubs them together briskly and begins again his journey to the sack with a flourish of his hands that lets you know a magician is at work. I had gone with my class at school to see the Atlanta Symphony play once, and the way Mr. Julian whisks his hands around reminds me of the conductor of the symphony. Except then it had been music the whirling hands brought forth. This time it will be a head.

Mr. Julian's hands fluff something midway the journey down into the sack. Then, straining with all his might, he begins lifting an object as heavy as the world. I look quickly at my grandmother. *If she screams her* woo-woo-woo's, I think, *I'll probably faint and miss the whole thing.*

Very arduously, by her blond hair, Mr. Julian lifts out a woman's head. No blood, I note right off the bat. No stringy muscles dangling. Why am I not surprised? I grin.

"What d'ya think, Mrs. Morgan?" Mr. Julian holds the head high so Louie can see. "Louie?"

Louie cheers in Spanish, and Grandmorgan, who has thrown her hands up at the sight of the head, snatches Betsy Manikin's oatmeal-box head off so fast I can't believe how quickly she becomes headless.

It takes Mr. Julian a few minutes to secure Louise's head in place with some tape he's brought for that purpose. By that time I have come close enough to see that it is the head of a store-window manikin. I glance at Louie. He's grinning and having a ball.

"What d'ya think?" Mr. Julian asks me.

I look back at Betsy and grin and nod. "Except," I say, reaching to touch her hair, "she doesn't look like a 'Betsy' now. She's . . . Aunt Pittypat from *Gone with the Wind,* with her tight curls." Mrs. Findley had taken Grandmorgan and me to see the movie when it came to town once.

"Hm-m-m." That pricks Mr. Julian's interest. "What d'ya think, Louie, my friend?" He picks up Betsy and carts her across the room, holding her at an angle so Louie can see.

Louie frowns. "Venus de Milo to me. No arms. Just long empty sleeves."

Mr. Julian rolls Betsy back to her customary place. "I don't know. Mrs. Morgan?"

"Betsy," Grandmorgan says, crossing her arms stubbornly. "Still Betsy."

"Well," Mr. Julian says, "a person who makes something owns the right to name it. She named *you,* didn't she, Louie?" He heehaws a loud laugh and plops down in the chair.

"But not 'Louie,'" I hop in to say. "She named him a name that belongs to a . . . a gangster or a person from Mars or somewhere. She named him a name nobody else ever heard of, not on earth."

"And?" Mr. Julian asks.

"She named him *Nym Hurt!*"

Mr. Julian lifts his head almost as though to catch a whiff of the name. He savors it a moment, then says, "A beautiful name," except he doesn't say 'beautiful' like people from Georgia say it. When Mr. Julian says the word, it comes out, "Be-*yow*-ti-ful!" and he shakes his head with the force of the word.

"Beautiful," Grandmorgan echoes and when my grandmother says it, I can hear the dry, wet way her mouth moves around it, holding it gently before it emerges soft and shaped by Georgia.

"And if a person is named 'Nym Hurt,' does one call him both names or shorten it to a nickname?" Mr. Julian asks.

It is my Uncle Louie who answers, being it is his name under discussion.

"Shorten it," he says. "To Louie."

Mr. Julian blinks. I don't see how "Louie" comes from "Nym Hurt" either, but Mr. Julian is too polite to ask.

We never call him "Nym Hurt," except for Grandmorgan now and then. Always call him "Louie," but, after Mr. Julian has said the name is beautiful, I begin to see that it just might be. The *m*-sound on the end of a word sort of rounds it off to a hum. And "Hurt" sort of slashes you when you say it. When I climb the mimosa tree, I say to the yard, "Nym Hurt, Nym Hurt," over and over, like a Trappist monk chanting a daily prayer.

But even with her new head, Betsy stays Betsy.

7

No one has said beans about Louray and her visit to try to get money. Louie certainly doesn't bring it up. Grandmorgan probably didn't hear what went on, and I'm certainly not going to tell her. But it rankles inside me like vinegar in sweet milk. Even when I'm not thinking about it, I *am*. The slightest thought of Louray makes me so mad I almost get sick to my stomach. Here the three of us have cut back to eating meat only twice a week to save on the grocery bill, and Louray leaves Windsor Castle to come clean across town to ask Louie for money. I'd be ashamed if it'd been me; I know that much.

I'm feeding Louie his dinner one evening when he tells me what happened during Louray's visit. He doesn't just out and out *say* it. He relays something else, and later, when I put two and two together, I know what he's really told me.

We've gotten through the nightly Spanish conversation and are talking about the war going on.

"You know what I heard in school last winter?" I ask.

He waits, so I continue. "Our teacher said it was so cold in the Ukraine, that when soldiers died, their frozen corpses were used to hold up the tents."

"Hm-m-m-m. Doesn't surprise me. Frozen human posts," he says. "A final use of manpower. I read that in the newspaper, come to think of it. It was true."

"That's horrible," I say, stirring his mashed-up crookneck squash.

"Oh, in war you learn to use everything, even your dead. And you know they would want you to."

"It makes me so mad! The whole war! I pray every night," I tell him, "that God will bless Hitler and kill him."

Louie laughs. "News reports say he's already dead, if you can believe them."

"They haven't found a body yet," I'm quick to say.

"You're covering all your bases, aren't you?"

"Why not? He's human like us, but he ordered

horrible things to be done. Those people we see pictures of in the evening *Journal* . . . he may as well have killed them. Standing there staring like they're dead inside."

Louie clears his throat. "In war, horrible acts occur on both sides. It's not clear cut, Shanta. Never all black and white . . ."

"We don't go round torturing and starving . . ."

"Hey!" He holds up one hand. "We do just as bad. Last February the Allies — that's us, the, in quotes, good guys — bombed the German city of Dresden."

"So?" I spoon in diced-up asparagus. "Hitler's German. He's head of the whole German nation."

"Now wait," Louie says. "Listen. Black and white would say, 'Good! All Germans are bad guys.' But that's not so. The Allies said we were hitting Dresden because of the Military Transport Center there. Fine! Hit it and leave. But no. Over a thousand planes bombed that city. A *thousand* planes."

He sips water from the glass straw.

"We got the Military Transport Center, all right. We also got citizens — adults and children. Museums full of irreplaceable art. Churches. Cathedrals. Dresden is flat. Wiped out, last February, and we, the *good guys,* did it."

I spoon in the rest of the mashed potatoes and think about Atlanta and the air raid warnings when we put blackout paper over the kitchen window and turned out the lights in the rest of the house. Huddled in there until the *all clear* whistle blew. I think how it might have been us instead of Dresden.

"No war," Louie says, wiping his mouth with his napkin to signal he is through, "private or global, is ever clear cut, is ever without innocent people being crushed."

"Well, what can we do," I ask, "if no war is fair?"

He wads the napkin into a tight ball and puts it carefully on the tray. "The trick, whether you win or lose, is to survive with honor. Don't lose that. If honor is all you have left, the trick is to hold it tight and not let it become a casualty of the war."

When I take the tray back to the kitchen, Grandmorgan snatches the dishes off it like she is boiling mad.

"Did I do something wrong?" I ask her, standing the tray on its end between the cabinet and the vegetable stand.

"What?" Grandmorgan looks over at me. "No." She blows a hard breath. "It just makes me madder than hops every time I think of the gall . . . of the nerve it took for Louray to come here and ask Louie . . . and tell him . . ."

She sputters away, masked by the sound of the running water. She had been canning vegetables for the winter ahead when Louray came, but she had apparently overheard enough to burn her up. This is the first time it has boiled over inside her and on out into her conversation.

"And he won't discuss it," she goes on. "Me, I'd have called the police to her. All he says is that it's *her* point of view. Reminds me of the way he used to defend the official when he played basketball in high school. He'd tell me after a game, 'Well, Mother, that's the way *he* saw it,' when one would call a foul on him in error."

I watch her fuming her way past the after-dinner chores.

"Well," I say, "I'll bet she won't come again."

"She'd better not!" Grandmorgan spits the words out hard and flat. "Because I'm not the good sport Louie is. He can't help what's happened. He's just as innocent as that there Honey is, and Louray's so hard-hearted she'll not even bring the child to see her own father."

Later, in bed, I can hear Fibber McGee and Molly coming from the radio in Louie's room.

"¡*Hasta Mañana!*" Louie calls to me from his room during a commercial. He knows I'm listening, too. Has turned the radio up loud enough for me to hear.

But I'm too relaxed to speak Spanish. "See you tomorrow, too," I manage and am just drifting past the night, leaving Atlanta behind, when it comes to me. Louie had told me what happened with Louray.

She left mad, I was betting. Had stayed a good hour, probably pleading and arguing. But Louie must have stood his ground . . . quiet, not shouting, but solid. When she saw she couldn't get what she came for, she had walked away. Walked away from her husband lying flat on his back, who had lost an awful lot of things, but honor was not one of them.

8

If I read it in the morning Constitution, *I think, then it must be true. I'm saving my money.* I reread the advertisement:

LYDIA E. PINKHAM'S VEGETABLE COMPOUND IS MADE ESPECIALLY FOR WOMEN, TO HELP RELIEVE PERIODIC PAIN WITH WEAK, NERVOUS, BLUE FEELINGS . . .

Grandmorgan comes into the kitchen. "Finish your yegg, Shanta," she says. "Mrs. Findley's taking us to the Frances Virginia Tearoom for lunch today. I want you to be hungry, so eat now . . . early on. It's a once-in-a-lifetime opportunity."

"Why's she taking us?"

"It's my seventieth birthday and she's celebrating it by buying us lunch."

"I didn't know it was your birthday. What about Louie?" I ask. Birthdays have never been different from any other day at Grandmorgan's house, but leaving Louie out would be unforgivable.

"We'll be bringing back a little napkin of goodies for him."

"Listen, Grandmorgan," I say, "it says right here in the *Constitution* that this stuff will build up resistance. Take away blue feelings."

"What stuff?"

"Lydia Pinkham's Vegetable Comp. . ."

"Take away the blues, huh?"

" 'And nervous feelings,' " I read aloud, thinking of how we all are feeling pretty nervous these days.

"Oh mercy, Shanta. I wish it were that simple."

"It says right here . . . see?"

"Yes, I see," she says, looking over my shoulder. "I also see the malaria mosquito is after *you*. Now you tell me—"

"Where?"

"Right there. Farther down the page." She shows me and then she looks right at me. "Now you tell me, how many malaria mosquitoes have you seen recently?"

I shrug I don't know.

"That's right. You don't know. Wouldn't know a malaria mosquito from a reg'lar one, would you?"

I shake my head no.

"Nor would I. Now don't you be believing ever thing you read or see, Shanta. Things aren't always what they seem. Every mosquito doesn't carry malaria."

I finish my egg, close up the newspaper, and run it on up to Louie so he can read it from cover to cover. As I trot through the house I think how glad I am I didn't waste my saved two dollars and forty-seven cents on vegetable compound.

I choose a striped chambray dress from my closet and am ready, along with Grandmorgan, at least thirty minutes early.

"Don't want to keep anybody waiting," Grandmorgan says as we sit in Louie's room expecting Mrs. Findley to honk in the driveway before long. "Now, Hurt . . ."

I look up at the sound of the name. And for the first time, it strikes me that the name describes exactly what he must feel.

"Now, Hurt, I've arranged for Lelia next door to slip over and stay and visit while we're gone. Emergency numbers are right by the phone in the hall. We'll probably be a couple of hours."

"I'll be all right," he protests.

"Just the same, Lelia's coming. You want me to

101

have a nice, relaxing seventieth birthday celebration, don't you?"

"Sure I do, Mother—"

"Well then, please me this way by letting Lelia stay to catch the phone or the door."

"Where you going?" he asks in a minute.

"The Frances Virginia Tearoom. Mrs. Findley says it's elegant. I guess elegance is about due when you turn seventy."

"What's 'elegance'?" I ask her.

Grandmorgan thinks on it. I can tell by the wait that "elegance" isn't familiar to her either.

"It's fancy . . . and smooth."

"Definitely not McGolphin," I say.

Louie brays out a laugh. "You got that right. Wait till I tell McGolphin how you talk about him, Shanta."

"Well . . . you're right," Grandmorgan says to me and stands to check herself in the mirror. "Mrs. Findley says they've got silver compotes at the Frances Virginia, with peppermint ice cream for dessert," she says as she tugs her dress down over her thick middle. "And deviled crab . . ."

I have just puckered to ask, "Compotes?" when Mrs. Findley honks. I skitter across the drive to get Lelia, and we back out of the driveway in style. I haven't ridden in a car in so long I've forgotten what it's like.

The Frances Virginia Tearoom is on Peachtree

Street, directly across from the Wincauff Hotel and catty-cornered from Davison-Paxon's.

"We'll slip over there after lunch," Mrs. Findley says, pointing to Davison's on our way in, "and see if they have any good sales."

Grandmorgan nods it is a good idea, though I know for a fact there is no money for sales, good or otherwise.

"Stand up straight," Grandmorgan whispers in my ear while we wait in a marble hallway to go up to the tearoom.

When we step off the elevator, the smell of good food almost knocks us out. It's wonderful. Lemons and tartar sauce and roast beef. And coffee dark as chocolate and just as rich. What a very different world we step off into. And, like music, the low-key tinkle of silverware plays below the hum of voices talking gentle and happy to each other.

Grandmorgan deserves the Frances Virginia Tearoom, I think to myself. Anybody who lives to be seventy and hasn't come to this place deserves to, not one day later than seventy years of age.

"Right this way," a man dressed like a penguin sings.

When we sit, the man places small menus before us. The only other time I have seen a menu was once with Louie and Louray. But then the menu was large and hot pink in a cafe. This one is small and the color of a winter sunset. Pale.

103

"I recommend the deviled crab," Mrs. Findley says to the both of us. And that's what all three of us order. Mrs. Findley is right, too. Maybe eating it out of the little hard crab shell adds to its goodness and the fresh-made tartar sauce, but it probably doesn't need any help. It just naturally melts in our mouths.

I am just lifting my spoon for the most perfect part of the meal . . . the peppermint ice cream, and am seeing for myself what a silver compote really is, have cut into the cold, pink mound nestled in the tall metal cup and am bringing the spoon to my open mouth, when I see her. Louray.

My eyes have left off looking at the spoon because I already know where it's heading, and I look across at the penguin-man as he bows and welcomes Louray Benton Morgan along with a man in a gray suit. He is probably as old as Louray and handsome enough to be a movie star.

Louray doesn't see me. I hold the frozen spoonful on my tongue. Can't swallow.

Maybe he's a cousin, I tell myself. But, honestly, I can't imagine flirting with a boy cousin, if I had one, the way Louray is carrying on with this man.

I start to grab Grandmorgan's sleeve to get her attention and tell her, but Mrs. Findley is talking a mile a minute. "And I told my Harry, just sleep on your side. It's your back that makes you snore."

"Tell you what did the trick for me," Grandmorgan says. "I made J.B. use tape. Reg'lar. Every night like clockwork, he'd brush his teeth then slap a couple of pieces of tape on his mouth. Never snored a *z*. He'd just . . ."

They are safely in their pasts so I can watch this without being noticed and try to understand it. When Louray and the man sit, he holds her chair for her. I eat and watch. Louray chats along and smiles at him with her perfect teeth. I notice her hair is holding its curl good, though how she sleeps in those aluminum curlers I have never been able to understand.

The two of them are at a table by the side window, about five or six tables away. Grandmorgan and Mrs. Findley have their backs to them. I still can't figure whether to say anything to Grandmorgan or not. I eat my peppermint ice cream and think. Seeing Louray gives me a deep hurting for Honey. I remember more things I miss about her. The tickling of her hair as she switched it around. The smell she had of banana Popsicles and sweat. Her laugh, high and giggly. I miss watching Honey sit in Louray's lap and reach up with her hand and cup Louray's chin from underneath like she owned her and nobody better take her away.

Finally I decide. It won't do a bit of good to tell my grandmother. It will ruin her birthday and then Louie's day when we get home and tell him. Telling would be like Dresden. Like sending a thousand bombers to do a hundred-bomber job. Louray has already left . . . already bombed our city. Why flatten it? No, this will be my secret . . . to remember Louray by whenever I miss Honey too much. I will probably tell Dennie, but not Grandmorgan. Not Louie.

I have just taken my last mouthful of that cold peppermint when I look up at the same time Louray is scanning our part of the dining room. Our eyes lock. Of course I'm not surprised because I've been watching Louray right along. But is Louray ever surprised! Every bone in her face falls a good half inch, dragged down by her jaw. She just stares in stunned amazement.

Now, if I were Louray, I think, *I'd be surprised to see me in a place like the Frances Virginia Tearoom, too. Good grief! I'd be surprised to see me at the Krystal Hamburger place down the street. But the Frances Virginia Tearoom! I reckon she did start.*

I gaze at her steady, don't smile, just hold on to her eyes. Louray's face gets really red and she looks away first. *That's twice now,* I think. I have hung up on her first on the telephone and now I have stared Louray down.

And that's what happens to people, I tell her in my mind, *when they do hurtful things. They get bit back!*

It makes me mad that I don't have the courage to march over there and tell her that out loud. I would like to. Grandmorgan listens every afternoon to a program on the radio called *Stella Dallas*. I heard it one afternoon when I was sick and lying on Grandmorgan's bed, playing with my paper dolls. On the program a wife found out her husband was seeing another woman. That wife marched into the restaurant where the husband and his lady friend were eating and the wife dumped all of his dirty laundry right in the middle of the table with their food. It was wonderful, then and now, as I remember it. I wish I had that kind of courage.

I am so mad that day of the Frances Virginia I forget to ask Grandmorgan if we are going to take any food scraps to Louie. At the last minute I remember and slip two thin, rolled cookie things that came on the saucer beside the compote of ice cream into my purse . . . wrapped in my handkerchief. I know Louie can let them melt in his mouth and then swallow them down and enjoy them.

As we rise to leave, I notice that Louray drops something on the carpet and spends quite a while fishing for it underneath the long pink linen tablecloth.

At home, when I hand Louie the carefully preserved rolled wafers, he says, "*Gracias*."

"*De nada*. You're welcome." And I try to sound enthusiastic but I'm scraped empty inside.

"*Siéntate*," Louie says. So I do, sit with him while

he eats them and tell him about the smells and the food and almost everything at the Frances Virginia Tearoom.

Then I go into my room and close the door. I take off my striped chambray dress and hang it in the closet. Then, dragging a chair across the floor to the closet, I climb up and fish around at the back of a shelf until I feel a smooth brown envelope. Large. Bulky. I take it and climb down and sit on the bed to open it.

Carefully, I slide out the folded blue velvet hat that Louray had worn for her wedding. I roll a small glass bead on its thread with my finger and remember the day in its entirety. How Grandmorgan and I had gotten up early to bathe and Grandmorgan had even curled my hair. How pure happiness had filled us all that morning. The world would never be the same again. We had been sure of it. And now, here it was — worse, less, not empty but awful.

I stiffen my shoulders in resolve and slide the hat back inside the envelope. Crossing to my desk, I staple the open end shut tight. A thousand staples. Still in my slip, I go out the other door of my room, not through Louie's room, cart the big Atlanta phone directory back from beside the hall phone and copy down the address of Louray's parents on Druid Hills Drive onto the envelope. Write "Mrs. Louray Morgan" above the address.

This afternoon I will wait outside for the postman

when he makes his second round, the afternoon delivery, and I'll give him fifty cents for postage from my savings. Surely that will be enough. The day, the memory, are all broken for me. The hat needs to be gone, too, so I won't stumble upon it years later and be ripped by the memory like by a stray splinter digging deep. It is better for Louray to have the hat back. And when she opens this large envelope with no return address, she'll understand the whole of it. She'll know that I want no part of her. But Honey. Honey is a different matter. Missing Honey will probably never stop.

Later that afternoon I tell Dennie and Earl all that happened.

"Well," Dennie says when I have finished, "deviled crab and peppermint ice cream ain't all the Frances Virginia Tearoom has to offer."

"And elegance," Earl chimes in, remembering how I had stressed that. "Don't forget elegance."

We laugh. Dennie and I. And Earl, hungry for laughs, pounds his leg with the flat of his hand and stomps his foot. I guess he is the object of more jokes than he tells.

"Roy," I tell him, "you are right about that." And feeling bold and dangerous in my anger, I add, "Elegance up to your bad ass."

He stops laughing.

"What's your bad ass?"

Dennie and I bend double we laugh so hard.

"I guess it's . . . your armpit," I finally tell him when I catch my breath. A lie, but easier than the truth.

Earl leaps to his feet and folds his arms so that each hand is hiked under an armpit.

"Up to my bad ass," he sings, strutting all across the yard.

Dennie shakes her head. "Aren't we all," she says. "Maybe even on beyond our bad asses. All the way up to our ears."

"Right," I say and wonder if Dennie means up to our ears in elegance or maybe something else. Something dark and not smooth like elegance, but hurtful and sharp. Like what had happened that day with Earnestine being slapped. I think about things not being what they seem. Or worse, things being all of what they seem, and more.

9

The Wednesday after the Frances Virginia Tearoom we all get into a hot game of Monopoly. There are Dennie and Earl and their next oldest sister Elizabeth and me. Since it's pouring rain, we are playing at the kitchen table in Dennie's house, which shocks me. I've never been allowed inside their house before.

I have just sold all of my green property to Elizabeth to stay afloat, but it doesn't look hopeful. Elizabeth takes a sip of lemonade and asks, "How come you call your grandmother *Grandmorgan?*"

Elizabeth is bossier than Dennie. By far. She is a take-charge person from the first throw of the dice. And, while Dennie and Earnestine must have their father's looks, his darker skin and hair, Elizabeth leans more toward her mother. She isn't as short. Is chubbier, but has a set about her jaw that I know she got, either passed on through kinship or from living with her mom. I watch her, fascinated. Somebody fifteen years old usually isn't as sure of herself as Elizabeth is.

"I don't know," I say. "That's the name she came with. And, anyway, it works out because she *is* Mrs. Morgan."

Elizabeth laughs. "Probably, you tried to say *grandmother* when you were little and that's what came out. Earl tried to say my name . . ."

I glance at him to see if he'll bleat out "Roy" to correct her, but the story is evidently fascinating to him so he keeps still.

". . . and it always came out *La Bethy*. That was after he had the steel plate put in."

"How'd that happen?" I ask, then land on Free Parking and collect the jackpot. "Hot dig! I need every bit of this and more."

"I don't know," Elizabeth says in answer to my question. "I wasn't old enough."

"Mama says I fell," Earl tells her.

"Then . . . he fell." Elizabeth rattles the dice in her hand and tosses them.

I scoot my chair forward so I can see where Elizabeth will land.

"Don't!" Elizabeth whispers, harsh.

"Don't what?"

"Scoot your chair across the linoleum. It'll scratch it."

I look down to see if I've left a mark. Nothing. I breathe a sigh of relief because their mother comes in to work at the sink just at that moment.

"We all the time scoot our chairs," I say low to Dennie. "Now I'll have to look for marks when I go home."

Dennie doesn't answer. She looks uncomfortable. Taking her turn, she passes GO, gets her two hundred dollars from Elizabeth, who is banker, then glances over at her mother. I watch her watch her mom. I look over at Mrs. Walling's back. She has tightly curled hair for about a third of the way up her head, then the top is flat, sloped but flat. She holds her shoulders as stiff as her hair, unnatural. The way she isolates herself from this roomful of people she could be in Savannah . . . or Rome, Georgia.

"What?" I mouth, catching Dennie's attention with a nudge.

But Dennie only shakes her head and goes back to playing. By lunch, I have gone bankrupt and am coaching Earl to keep him afloat.

"It's time to stop, Dennie," Mrs. Walling says from where she has been making rolls beside the sink. Her voice is flat, and if she'd just said Christmas was tomorrow you still wouldn't be excited.

"Why don't we remember where we each are and fold up the board," I suggest. "We could make sandwiches and play all afternoon in my living room or on my front porch. It's wide enough the rain won't spatter on us."

Dennie looks across at her mother. "Okay, Mom?"

The kitchen is sort of dark with only the one light bulb hanging down over where we're playing and her mother is working in a dim area. It is like her mind can't see to answer. *Good grief,* I think, *it's free. And it isn't like Dennie is leaving for the week. Just an afternoon.* But apparently it's a hard decision.

Finally Mrs. Walling nods. We're writing down who owns what property and putting everybody's money in separate envelopes so we can start where we left off when Earl accidently elbows the bank box, upsetting all the rest of the money.

"Uh-oh," he sings out loudly. Nothing about Earl is ever quiet. "We're up to our bad asses in money now. Uh-oh!"

Dennie and I sputter a laugh, but Elizabeth knows. In one swift stride Mrs. Walling is over top of Earl, yanking him up by the arm.

"What did you say?" It's said so low it's hard to hear, but the force is there. It's like Mrs. Walling has been walking a thin wire all morning and suddenly has fallen off. She's going to take us all with her, too.

114

"Mom," Elizabeth stands quickly, "he doesn't know what it means. Please. He doesn't understand . . ."

Earl is stiff, standing like somebody has shouted, "FREEZE!"

"Here, Earl," Elizabeth keeps on, "reach down here and help me pick up all this money. It's a mess."

I really think Elizabeth is trying to distract Mrs. Walling more than she is Earl. It works. The woman shifts her attention from Earl to the scattered money. Looking back at him she says, "Help Elizabeth pick up the money then," and leaves the room.

Earl watches her go. Then, stooping to work with Elizabeth, he whispers, "Definitely a mess. Definitely up to our bad asses."

Nobody laughs. When I leave, Elizabeth is making him promise never to say that again. I know I won't ever say it again. And it goes without saying, they can't come over for Monopoly.

It's just as well. If they had come, they might have heard Louie tell his dirty joke. I hear it because when I come onto the porch, I sit out there to unwind from all the tensions across the street. Lean against the brown stone wall of the house and sit right down on the cool tile outside the door of Louie's room that opens onto the porch.

McGolphin, apparently home on a lunch break from Sears and Roebuck where he works, has come over to show Louie a trick he has bought. They are planning to spring it on Grandmorgan.

"See, here's where it is," I hear him tell Louie. "Right acrosst here. It's smooth as glass. An invisible lid. She'll never see it. But come time for her to eat her oatmeal of a morning, why it'll roll right off this spoon. We'll get Shanta to slip it to the table."

They both chuckle and I prick up at the mention of my name. So I am listening full steam ahead when Louie says to McGolphin, "Hey, Herb told me a good joke the other night."

"Yeah? What?"

"Well, there were a bunch of old geezers sitting on the front porch of a hotel, rocking and jawing, when, lo and behold, two old ladies run by, naked as jay birds."

Lord, help us, I think, *they don't know I'm here. Nothing to do but sit tight and pray this'll be quick. Too late to struggle up and away and not much chance of doing it quietly.*

Louie keeps rolling. " 'D'you see that?' one fellow turned and said to the guy sitting next to him. 'Sure did.' 'Well what d'ya think it was?' 'Not rightly sure but it set off a burning desire inside; that's for certain.' 'A burning de-sire?' 'Yes, indeed. Made me want to race inside and plug in a iron, they was so wrinkled.' "

Louie and McGolphin cackle. *It could be worse,* I think, sitting there. But it is peculiar to me how I

116

had been developing a person along in my mind until that person hadn't a fault in him. Then along comes reality and you find out he's just as human as anybody else.

I sit on the porch a while and think about Louray and Honey. Think how it might be to have a husband who can't get out of bed. Probably can't set any burning fires in bed, either. What little I know of that lends itself to say that the bedroom is important to a marriage. And to have a daddy who can't take you anywhere. Ever. Louie surely isn't a saint, and surely has his problems, but he does still love them, I'm sure of it.

I might do a lot of things, I think, *if I were a wife and that happened to my husband, but, honest to God, I couldn't just leave somebody for good. Not forever.*

10

You don't have to be a genius to know that something isn't quite right across the street at the Wallings. Mrs. Piersey is odd, staying inside all the time with friends and neighbors stopping by to run errands for her. But that's odd, not wrong. The Wallings have something wrong going on. Not their overzealous focus on material things either, and their upkeep. It goes deeper than that. I read it in Dennie's eyes. There is fear there. And Earl's eyes. His eyes are different from Dennie's. They're beginning to wear a glazed, faraway look a lot of the time. He just checks out for a little while, now and then, and we have to bring him back to our games.

That day we played Monopoly was the last time

I saw the Earl I had come to know. When I think back on it later, I realize that for the rest of the summer he acts strange. Doesn't want to play Roy Rogers, even. Just sits dull as a snail, and moody, like he's pulled back into his shell, quiet. My theory is that Mrs. Walling needs Lydia Pinkham's Vegetable Compound more than any other woman in the city of Atlanta. And is probably too strict on them all, especially Earl. But I wonder if that's all there is to it.

It is the first Saturday of August when I begin a course that will ultimately lead to the discovery of the truth. The war in the Pacific is still on, even though Ike came home to the big parade in New York City back in June for his part in the war in Europe. Louie and I have many long discussions about Ike's homecoming and what the future holds for him. Louie says Ike will be president one day because he's such a hero. I say not. Just because he can lead an army doesn't mean he'll make a good president.

"I like Truman," I vow that night at supper as I feed Louie. "And Margaret. She sings and he plays the piano."

"And that makes a good president?" Louie is feisty as ever. Lying in bed isn't easing off his spunk any. "Playing the piano and having a daughter make like a canary? Harry Truman will endorse Ike next go-round. You wait and see."

We go round and round.

When I finish feeding him supper, that fourth day of August, the magicians start arriving. No kids, so I hightail it across the street to see if Dennie and Earl can play. Just as I hit their curb the girls all burst out of their front door on the move, their mother going at a dead run out in front of them all.

"Hi," I call.

Dennie doesn't stop. Doesn't slow down, even. She yells over her shoulder, "I can't play. Go home."

Mrs. Walling even starts the car before all the doors are shut and shoots them backwards out of the driveway and off.

I wander on back across the street and, taking a small chip of rock at the end of the driveway, I scratch out a hopscotch map on the sidewalk. Then, tossing the rock chip into the first square, I begin a game of solitaire hopscotch.

The preacher's boy, Ralph Edward Weathers, rides by on his bike. "Hey," he slows down to call, then circles back like he's looking at something. Here it comes. I brace myself, but all he says is, "There's a string or something hanging down from your shorts."

I look down but don't see anything.

"It's right there . . . on the left side. It's a string. Oh! No!" He claps his hand over his mouth in mock horror. "Sorry, it's your leg."

Laughing like a hyena, he bucks his bike for joy and rides on down the street.

"What a jerk!" I say out loud and keep on with my game. *If he counts that as a get-back, he's losing his thunder.*

The magicians start leaving along about dark. Dennie hasn't come home yet. Since it's getting too dark to see the hopscotch map, I give it up and sit on the steps next to the petunia pots. The smell is even sweeter than honeysuckle, and I drink it in like it's cold tea, brimful of ice and lemon and mint leaves.

I hear Grandmorgan come out and put the change for the bread man underneath the board on the inner porch ledge. I hear the screen door close behind her. And then I hear a dog howling. I look up at the moon, wondering if that's what made the dog start up.

After about five minutes, I decide it isn't a dog after all. It sounds like it might be something out back in Dennie's yard. I walk down the steps and cross the street, stopping at the end of the Wallings' driveway. It surely does sound like an animal crying out in back of her house somewhere. I stand in the driveway debating whether or not to track the sound. It's getting awfully dark, even with the streetlights, and, after all, this isn't out in some swamp. Other people will hear it and check on it, if need be.

With that decision made, I turn to recross the street when I hear a man's voice.

"What're you doing in my yard?"

I look up. It has come from a really tall man standing in Dennie's side yard next to the Warnocks' house. It's dark but from what I can see I guess he might be one of the two men who had been out in front on the Walling's moving-in day. The one who yelled at Earl. The one I think is their daddy.

"I was waiting for Dennie," I answer him, leaving out the dog part.

"Well, don't. She'll not be here for quite a while. You may as well go on home."

I turn to do so when he asks in a voice that comes out mostly growl, "Where do you live?"

Something in me instinctively hates and fears this person. I could answer. Should, I guess. But I don't. Just cross the street silently to my curb and start up my front yard steps.

"I ast you a question," he shouts, but I keep on walking.

If he didn't know before, he'll know now by the house I go into, I think suddenly. But it is too late. *That's right. And now he knows where I live.*

"Is your daddy the tall man or the short one?" I ask Dennie two days later.

"Why?" I shrug. "He's tall. The other 'un is my Uncle Stuart, my mother's brother."

"Why'd you leave so fast the other night?" The second question comes almost before Dennie has answered the other. This is the first time I have seen her since, but I've been wondering about it.

"Went on a errand."

"What kind?"

No answer. Dennie just scratches the dirt by her front steps with a twig.

"Where?"

"Why are you so nosy?" Dennie looks up at me when she asks.

It takes me back. "Well, I didn't mean to be. It's just that . . . I thought I heard a dog yowling in your back yard so I crossed over, going to check on it. Then, decided better . . ."

Dennie watches me like she wants to be sure of every word I say. "So?"

"Well . . . I was crossing back over when a tall man in overalls asked me what I was doing."

"It was my daddy."

Her eyes shift to the air above the sidewalk, sidewalk hot enough to cook a whole meal on. In fact, little squiggles of torrid air seethe above it out toward the street. The only sound for a few minutes is a bird in a nearby bush in Mrs. Piersey's yard. Calling like it's a rubber band or a nerve snapping. Not expecting an answer. Just calling.

Finally, I ask, "Is something wrong at your house, Dennie?"

She doesn't look over at me but she does leave off staring at the sweltering air. She looks down to where she is gouging the driest dirt in America. "Families don't talk about themselves," she says low.

"What?" I laugh. "When they say, 'Loose lips sink ships,' Dennie, they're talking about war. They're not talking about this kind of thing. It's okay to tell a friend."

"I don't think so."

"Heck," I'm back at her in no time, "well no, not to just anybody. But to a good friend . . ."

Dennie shakes her head.

"I tell you about us. About Louray at the Frances Virginia Tearoom and about . . ."

"That don't count. You're not a family."

If Dennie had fired a gun at me, it couldn't have hurt more. What she says hits the most vulnerable spot inside me. Dennie could say many things, even hateful words, and they wouldn't hurt me nearly as bad as saying we aren't a family. I've been afraid of that all along, the not-a-family thing. And here it is. True. We're nothing more than a farm team. Never going to make the majors.

At first I'm too stunned to move. Then anger comes and takes over my whole body, bowing it rigid and electric.

"What?" I stand up it makes me so mad. My legs tremble with rage, but I stand in the front walk square where my feet had started out when I sat down.

"You heard me. You're not a family."

"We are, so. What are we if we're not a family?"

Dennie looks up and says, "Lucky."

I carry *lucky* with me as I stalk across the street. I don't even look at the word until I am high in the mimosa tree. Then I examine it, relax enough that I think it odd, finally, that Dennie would say people without family are lucky.

Later that evening I ask Grandmorgan, "Are we a family?"

Grandmorgan chews her dentures for a minute. "You might say that," she finally says.

"But there's not a father and a mother," I argue Dennie's side of the issue.

"Doesn't have to be." Grandmorgan is sorting scraps for a quilt at the kitchen table. "Whyn't I wait till there was daylight enough to see to do this? Tell me, Shanta, is this yere navy blue or black?"

"Navy."

"Good." She folds the cloth into a small square and plops it into a baby food jar she has saved from the two-week stint of Louie's baby-food diet.

"How can we be a family?" I push on.

Grandmorgan slaps a piece of cloth down on the oilcloth table cover and looks across at me. "Are you complaining?"

I am baffled. "No. Want to know. That's all."

"Well, here it is, once and for all. A family is those who live under the same roof, who are joined by the same effort. It could be twelve cats and a man. Could be a half a dozen chil'ren and their mama. Or, it could be a old woman, a man taken to his bed, and a young'un. We're a family, Shanta. Take my word for it."

"But what are we joined by?"

Grandmorgan doesn't hesitate a second. "By the urgency to survive, child. By the joy of knowing another person up close. By a good cry now and then. And a good laugh. Always a good laugh."

The more I think about what she says, the more I know she's right. Dennie's saying we aren't a family doesn't make it *so*. I begin to believe we might be a family, especially if laughing is what holds a family together. A couple of days later Louie has Grandmorgan down on her hands and knees under the foot of his bed getting set for a big laugh on McGolphin and the magicians and anybody else who might happen by.

"Okay, Hurt," she calls from where she is kneeling on the hard wooden floor. She is calling him *Hurt* more often these days. "I still don't see why Shanta couldn't have done this."

"I'm afraid she'd not be able to get it right," he calls back. "*¡Escucha!* Listen! Now squeeze some of that cement glue from that tube right onto the floor."

"It'll remove the paint."

"Who cares. Squeeze it."

She does. A big blob of it right on the dark painted floorboard.

"Now what?"

"D'you squeeze it?"

She nods.

"D'you squeeze it?"

"Yes!" she screeches, miffed at being down at that angle. "I nodded."

"I can't see you nod, Mother. *Perdón,*" he adds as an afterthought.

"All right all right. What's next?"

"Take the quarter and lay it right on the glue. And listen now. *¡Importante!* Don't mash it because the glue'll squirt out around the edges and give it away."

"Done," she croaks.

"Did you mash it?"

"No!"

"That's it then," Louie says. "*Gracias.* When it dries, we'll try it out."

"Now comes the hard part," Grandmorgan tells me, backing out from beneath Louie's bed. "Getting up."

I help her up. After lunch we give the quarter a test. Louie has me put a handful of small change folded in his sheet by his legs. Since they are paralyzed stiff, he can't kick it. But his arms are strong and can yank the sheet and spill the change everywhere. It works. When I pick up all the money, the quarter sticks solid to the floor.

The first victim is Mrs. Soap-Opera Paige from down the street. We have it all planned out it will be one of the magicians so when the knock at the front screen comes, Louie calls out, "Come on in," thinking it's one of his buddies. He yanks the sheet hard. Money goes everywhere.

"Lord love a duck," Mrs. Paige squawks and sails in his room to help him.

Women don't all the time crawl around under beds, especially older women wearing girdles Playtex invented to keep a person from moving. Grandmorgan just thought she had a hard time getting back up. I'm convinced we're going to have to hire help to dislodge Mrs. Paige. I go down with her to speed up the works and cover up the quarter so she won't see it and drag this out. I'm not sure she even remembers how to laugh, and I don't want to have to teach her all over again.

" 'S that it?" she keeps asking, rotating her head like a cow looking for a fresh spot of grass.

"Yes ma'am," I say, making sure I'm covering the quarter.

"Well, now then," she begins and I know we are in for hard times. "My rheumatism may never let me up. That and the headache I'm working on."

Most people would back on out and then hang on to the bed to pull themselves up by. Not Mrs. Paige. She backs clear across the room. Grandmorgan and I watch in fascination.

"What's she doing?" Louie keeps whispering to Grandmorgan, but she's too intrigued to answer.

When Mrs. Paige reaches the door, she hauls herself up by the doorknob mostly. I run to steady the door so it won't swing around while it's bearing all her weight and flip her clear out of Fulton County.

Thank goodness she's nearsighted and can't see the quarter still stuck to the floor up under the bed.

When Herb Hunter comes that night, Louie calls Grandmorgan on the intercom so she won't miss it after all her hard work. I stay to see the fun, too, although I wonder if we'll ever top Mrs. Paige, who left thinking she'd done her good deed for the week, picking up all that change.

Herb has brought his two girls, Patsy and Beverly. When Louie gives that sheet what-for, money goes everywhere. Herb is on his hands and knees faster than a cat after a mouse. He lies flat on his stomach to rescue the change that has rolled way up under the bed. Patsy and Beverly are right down there with him, raking in money as fast as they can.

Herb crawls back down toward the stuck quarter.

When he gets to it, he picks at it and moves on toward the nickel beside it before he realizes he hadn't gotten the quarter.

"What the hay?" he mumbles, going back for it.

Louie looks across at me and Grandmorgan and winks. We've raised the head of his bed up a little so he can see better.

Herb works on that quarter a full minute before it comes to him something is up. He wiggles out from under the bed and sits back on his heels, looking at Louie, who is doing his best to hold in a laugh.

"Louie, buddy," Herb says, "you've got one mighty peculiar quarter here."

Grandmorgan chuckles out loud. Herb Hunter looks her way and that's when he knows he's been had.

Well, Herb Hunter is funny and so is Harold Hendrix. None of them as funny as Mrs. Paige in my book. But we're all waiting for McGolphin. He doesn't come by every single day. By the time McGolphin shows up, it is August sixth and the United States has flown an airplane named the *Enola Gay* to a place called Hiroshima. The pilot's family lives right in Columbus, Georgia. Named Tibbits. He drops an atomic bomb they call "Little Boy."

Nobody feels like laughing. It's good that the war is probably going to be over, but I start thinking of people. Of Dresden. And Hiroshima is hundreds of times worse if you can believe the news reports. I think of families torn apart. It dwells inside me, this bombing, and goes with me everywhere.

McGolphin comes the night the news breaks and the four of us sit in Louie's room quiet and listen to the radio.

"I think we were right to do it," McGolphin finally says. "Looking at the pictures of the concentration camps, I'd say any peace is not better than any war." He sits for a minute. "And not done, we'd 'a' lost a hell of a lot of our own boys before it was over."

"You're right," Grandmorgan agrees. I'll bet she's thinking of Jimmy Piersey.

Louie just grunts. I wonder if he's remembering Dresden, the way I am. I wonder if he sees people like us burning, scalded by the blast. Nobody asks me for my two cents worth, and I'm glad. I can't get past the people.

"Hey," McGolphin says at one point, "you got a quarter down there on the floor, up under your bed."

"Never mind it," Louie tells him. "Just leave it. Mother'll get it when she dust mops."

And so it is days before McGolphin receives the joke.

Meanwhile, that night the news of the A-bomb broke, I begin the dreams. I haven't dreamed, that I can remember, in a long time. Oh, I would wake up of a summer morning all smiling inside like I'd just left a satisfying dream. But I was never sure if it was a dream that caused it or just the smell of Georgia's summer mornings filling me. Petunia scent coming in my open window by the driveway. The smell of Lelia and Rowena Stewart's flowers rioting in their back yard.

But that night the awful dreams come. Maybe because of the bomb, but they aren't about the bomb. I see my mother running toward me. But instead of reaching me and hugging me, my mother sails right on past. It has been too long. She doesn't even recognize her own daughter.

I twist in agony against the pillow and fight to get the dream back so I can catch my mother.

And then comes the dream I never want back. Yet, night after night it is there . . . in the dark . . . in my mind. It is night. The sound comes again from behind Dennie's house. That dog howling. In my dream I creep across the street and down the drive beside the Wallings' house, careful to be on the lookout for Dennie's father. I am almost to the Wallings' back porch when I hear a hammering sound. Looking quickly to my left, I see that it is Mrs. Piersey frantically rapping on the kitchen window and pointing. Pointing. Where is she pointing? What does she mean? Her face is twisted in terror.

I look in the direction of Mrs. Piersey's finger. Back. Where I have just come from. Up the driveway toward my own house. Away from that horrible sound coming from the Wallings' back yard. And there he is, Mr. Walling, bearing down on me with a look on his face straight from the devil, himself.

I dart across Mrs. Piersey's back yard to lose him. Back up the other side of her house, across the street, and fly up my own front steps and into the house.

"*Buenas noches,*" Louie calls out cheerfully as I slam and lock the front door.

Ignoring him, I run to the hall, grab Grandmorgan's dust mop, and push up the trapdoor to the attic. I stand on the cedar chest and pull myself into the opening, drawing up the mop with me and closing the trapdoor lid back over the hole.

Then and only then, in this reoccurring nightmare, do I breathe one long sigh of relief. I'm only allowed one, because I hear and remember at the same time. I have forgotten to lock Louie's porch door and every single time I dream it I forget that. As I remember that oversight, I hear Mr. Walling shouting at Louie. He is in the house, in Louie's room, and I feel the guilt I had felt over Louie's broken pitcher. Only a hundred times worse, and I am helpless. It is always at that precise moment in the dream that I awake.

I never find out what the howling sound is or if Mr. Walling kills Louie or if I, myself, die of heat prostration in the attic. Never find out nor want to.

In Georgia there's a weed, a vine, called kudzu. It grows all over Georgia. Out in the wilds. Unwanted, but there. I remember seeing it when we rode along the highway with Louie driving. In the early days when we had a car. I would watch the kudzu out the back window. Look at the shapes it made, covering the trees and old free standing farm buildings that nobody used anymore.

I think about those shapes one night as I'm trying to fall asleep. About how they used to scare me. Then I make the connection. Fear is like kudzu. It creeps on the outer places where you wander in your mind, away from busyness. Covering solid things, disguising them into grotesque shapes. I know I'm covered in the fear of being stalked. And the fear is so abundant, just like kudzu, it's beginning to consume me. Keeping me from the real world. In a way, I am almost as bound by the fear as Louie is by the arthritis.

11

I discover the picture by accident. Louie has taped it to an inside wall framing a shelf of his bedside table. An inside wall where only he knows it is there. But then I find it. Am dusting for Grandmorgan and suddenly there is this picture of Charles Atlas, scantily clad, his muscles bulging, a small cutout picture stuck to the wood with adhesive tape.

"What's this?" I stoop down to get a better view.

Louie gives a nervous laugh.

I look back up at him. I've heard about pinups inside soldiers' lockers. Pinups of Betty Grable and her famous legs. Rita Hayworth in a bathing suit. But why would Louie have a picture of Charles Atlas, the world's strongest man, taped to the inside of his table? I squat down and read aloud the name signed like an autograph across one corner of the bottom of the picture. "Charles Atlas."

"Okay," Louie says. "You've seen it. Now, if you'll stand up here so I can see you, I'll explain what it's doing there."

I stand and twist the dust cloth behind my back. Something not your business is often hard to hear.

"I'm reading a book." He points to it on the lower inner shelf, beside the slop jar where he relieves himself and which Grandmorgan empties faithfully after every meal. "It's about self-image. In a nutshell, if you hold in your mind a healthy image of yourself, hold it hard and fast, you will become it. So I put a picture up to remind myself. Stuck it up with tape so I can undo it and look at it to fill my mind."

I bring the dust cloth around and squat to dust the spring coils under Louie's hospital bed. Think and swipe. Look back at the book lying on top of the Bible he reads daily and next to the Spanish textbook.

"So," I rise to ask, "if you concentrate on that picture of a healthy man day in and day out, your body will automatically heal itself?"

Louie blinks for a nod and smiles. "*Sí.*"

"Do you honestly believe that?"

He blinks again. Lets his eyes stay shut a whole second to make it emphatic.

"What're those papers sticking out of the book?"

He opens his eyes. "My notes."

"Notes?"

"Yep. I've been listing all the joyful facts of my life. Then I go back over the list to remind myself of the reasons for joy."

"But what if it doesn't work?"

"You tend to become what you think and say, Shanta. Mind over matter works," Louie assures me.

"And what if it doesn't?" I am adamant. Sometimes, actually often, things don't work.

"What have you lost?" he asks with a firm smile, behind which rest no teeth, only gums.

And would staring at a picture of an Ipana toothpaste grin all day bring back your teeth? I am tempted to ask, but don't.

"What have you lost!" Louie says again but this time it isn't a question. And this time I finally have an answer. *Hope.* But I only say it to myself, not wanting to douse the only spark Louie might have.

12

Tuesday night it's hotter than ever in my bedroom. I've gotten up to use the bathroom one more time before going to sleep. On my way down the hall, I hear my grandmother's voice, talking to somebody. Pausing just before her bedroom door, I listen. She certainly isn't on the phone. The cord won't stretch that far. Is it McGolphin? Maybe through the window? But there is a singsongy rhythm to her words. I listen some more.

"D. Do unto others as you would have them do unto you. E. Evil men don't understand the importance of justice . . . F. For all things work together to the glory of God . . . G. Go ye into all the world and . . ."

I know now. It's a Scripture alphabet. Grandmorgan is saying it to get to sleep. I look in the door and see by the dim moonlight coming through the tall windows my grandmother lying on her back with her hands folded as though she is praying. These are harsh times and I guess she's doing what she knows to do to keep her peace. Louie is listing joy and Grandmorgan is remembering Bible verses.

"And it must work," I tell Dennie the next morning. "She doesn't get upset much except over Louray and the way she's treating Louie." We're sitting at the curb in the shade of Rowena Stewart's chinaberry tree. Earl doesn't want to play, so the three of us are sitting and eating Popsicles.

"It's her rosary," Dennie says, nodding like she knows. "Our grandmother is a Catholic and she says a rosary with beads to remind her what to say next."

"She does not," Earl shoots back. Mad and quick.

"She does so." Dennie raises her voice. "I oughta know. We visit her every week or two. You don't go with us, Earl."

"Is that where you go when you go on your 'errands'?" I'm quick to ask.

Dennie slides her eyes from Earl to me. She knows what I'm doing. So she answers with a question. "You're still trying to find out where we go, aren't you?"

But Earl hasn't let go of the argument. "No,

139

Dennie. She does not have bees telling her what to say!"

"Beads, Earl. Not bees. B–E–A–D–S."

He absorbs it, then snickers. "I knew bees couldn't talk."

Dennie shakes her head and makes a face at me. Earl is edgier than a bee in autumn, himself.

That evening we continue the conversation that is interrupted because Dennie's mother has chores for her and my dead granddaddy's social security check has come in the morning mail so I walk to the neighborhood grocery to help Grandmorgan carry the grocery sacks back home. The two of us haven't been gone to the grocery over three-quarters of an hour, but things aren't right when we get back. We can tell even from where we're walking on the front sidewalk. We can hear Louie groaning clear out there.

Grandmorgan hands me her two sacks and rushes up the front steps, leaving me to struggle in on my own. At the porch screen door, I set all four sacks down, then carry them one at a time back to the kitchen.

Grandmorgan stalks in behind me. "Just put the groceries on up, Shanta. Louie's sicker than a dog. I've got to call Dr. Emerson right away."

The doctor comes on his way home to lunch. Leaves Louie's room shaking his head.

"May be food poisoning or the summer flu," he tells Grandmorgan. "I'm not real sure. I'll send some pills for nausea over from the pharmacy. See if they help and keep me posted. If he's still nauseated tomorrow morning, we'll have to try something else."

He leaves and I listen to Uncle Louie fight the dry heaves all afternoon. No need to worry about feeding him supper this night. He can't even keep a drink of water down.

"Law, Hurt," I overhear Grandmorgan say at one point, "you didn't take too many Nembutal capsules, did you?"

He says, soft and tired, "No."

"You've not despaired beyond hope, have you?"

"No."

And I know that to be the truth. A person counting hard on mind over matter, thinking about joy, isn't about to take a handful of pills to end it all. And anyway, Louie and I have had long discussions about the Japanese kamikaze pilots and how they must be out of brains to go to certain death so willingly. Yes, I am *sure* it is food poisoning or the summer flu some visiting magician has brought unawares.

That evening finds Dennie and me back out at the curb, pulling little stems off fallen chinaberries. Earl is absent, a rare occurrence. We can hear Louie through his open porch door, still fighting and strangling with the dry heaves. Ralph Edward whizzes by on his bike. We hear him but don't even look up.

"I sure hope Louie doesn't die," I whisper, hugging my knees to my chest to be tight and less vulnerable to worry.

"Me, too," Dennie says. "And I've never even met your Uncle Louie, but I still hope not."

"If he lives, I'll take you inside and introduce you."

"Okay."

"If he does die, he'll go straight to heaven," I say. I know for a fact. There's probably not another person on the planet any better than Uncle Louie. When I was little and first came to live with them, he'd take me to the college library when he studied afternoons. I'd sit and look at magazines while he did his work. Then we'd always go for an ice cream cone. If ever a person would go straight to heaven, it would be Louie. I get a lump in my throat just thinking about it.

"No such place as heaven," Dennie says, lining chinaberries in a row at the curb edge.

"What did you say?"

"I said, there ain't no such place. Heaven is a pitiful dream people hold because living on earth is so bad there's gotta be something better, somewhere, sometime."

"Gosh, girl!" I look at Dennie hard. "You have sure got weird beliefs."

"No weirder than yours," she whips back. "I'll bet you believe in God, don't you?"

I look at the streetlight that has just come on. "Must be nine o'clock," I say, buying time for a good answer to give Dennie.

"You do believe in God, huh?" she persists.

"Well, if I believe in heaven it pretty much says I do. And you don't?"

Dennie shakes her head slow and knowing. "That's how people explain things they don't understand. God did it!"

"Listen, Dennie, I've had too many close calls. I know there's a God. One night before Louie got took by the arthritis, we were all riding out on the highway, me, and Louray who was pregnant with Honey, and Grandmorgan. Louie was driving. He took a wrong turn down a highway that was unfamiliar."

"Please don't tell me a tale of God jumping in his Superman suit and swooping down to save you from destruction," she says, scratching at a mosquito bite.

I just ignore her and go on with my story. " 'I can get us home,' he said. 'Trust me.'

"We rode in the dark. Grandmorgan used to say you always outdrive your headlights at night and

143

Louie did just that. Way off in the distance Grandmorgan spotted a train light.

"'Look-a-there,' she says, pointing. I can remember like it was last night.

"We all look and, after a minute, we begin to think the train and our car were heading toward the same spot in the road.

"'Louie!' my grandmother shouted, but it was too late. He couldn't have stopped if he had wanted to. He did the next best thing. He stomped it, just floored that accelerator. We didn't even touch those tracks, we flew across them so fast. And the train, whew! It whizzed on across right behind us, blowing its whistle like it was stuck."

I stop to remember how shaken we all were. "My grandmother talked for weeks about it. About the night we 'nearly got swept off the planet' she called it. 'How instantly a person can have the life ripped right from him,' she'd say. 'It takes nine months to form a life and in less time than it takes to hiccup, a person can leave for good. It's that close. Next door the whole time. Within view. Always.'"

"Hm-m-m-m-m," Dennie grunts.

I think she is impressed by the story, so I add, "Grandmorgan said God must have a special plan for all of us in that car that He was saving us for."

Dennie stands up to go, takes her bare foot and sweeps the row of chinaberries she has lined up from the curb into the street. "Right," she says to me.

Then looks up to my house. "Like stick your Uncle Louie in a bed for the rest of his life? Great plan! I'm sure I can't wait to see what He's got up his sleeve for me!"

There isn't an answer in my head.

I watch Dennie cross the street and disappear in the darkness of her front yard.

"Please, God," I whisper, "please don't let Louie die. I'll bargain anything. Do without. I'd rather Louie not die than the war be over. Take Jimmy Piersey instead of Louie. Take me. Please. *Por favor.*"

I sit for a long time, thinking about what Dennie has said. *Life on earth isn't all that bad,* I begin thinking. I mash a chinaberry between my thumb and forefinger. Sniff it.

Yuck. Why are you called chinaberry, anyway? Did you start out in China? Years and years ago? And somebody brought you to America? When? Who? Were you part of a plan, too? Or is this whole universe a handful of chinaberries thrown up in the air and flung into orbit by nobody in particular?

Windows up and down Clay Street are open against the heat that holds steady even if it *is* night. Fans try to suck in cooler air and blow out the hot. Through the windows of Dennie's house there comes the sound of heat. The kind of heat that boils inside a person mean enough to make the people around him hate earth and even life, itself. I listen

145

and think how hard it would be to have two mean parents. Not having either parent is bad enough. Now, here is something far worse than not having parents. *No wonder Dennie doesn't believe in God,* I think as I hear Dennie's father slit and stab the air with his sharp rod of a voice. *No wonder.*

13

We've dropped another A-bomb. This time on Nagasaki. America listens to its radios and waits. Meanwhile, the yard has grown four inches. Even with no rain the weeds still grow. Dry, stubborn weeds. I lean into the push mower. McGolphin sharpened its blades for me when he saw me struggling. Then he laid his file beside the petunia pots and went on inside to visit with Louie, who is out of the woods, the doctor said. Just the summer flu. Nobody else has gotten it. All that praying I'd put myself through, and it's just the flu. Or maybe *that* is the answer to the praying.

I push with my body and let my mind travel in other directions. I am deep in a war love story. The soldier I'm engaged to marry has returned on furlough and we're getting married tonight.

A piercing whistle begins to wedge its way into my consciousness.

"Whoo, doggie!" a voice calls after the whistle. "Hubba hubba!"

I never slow, nor look up. It is that hateful Ralph Edward Weathers again, this time circling his bike in the street and calling to me. I mow straight on down beside the curb, then back up toward Boulevard Drive. Down the next row . . .

"Where'd you get them Betty Grable legs? Hm-m-m-m-uh! Gorgeous, I'll say."

Oh, this week they're Betty Grable's? Last time you commented they were pieces of string. Stupid boy. I lean and mow and think to myself how next mowing I might just mow at an angle to make a pretty pattern. Like velvet, lawns have nap running one way and counter nap running the other. And I'll mow even later, when it's near dark, too.

Then in one bolt-swift slice of time, the preacher's boy finds himself in steely hands. The comment rising from the back of his throat never hatches. It's swallowed back down to lie alongside supper and pass out of his body along another avenue. But never from his mouth, because the head of the Walling household has seized all one hundred thirty pounds of mean and is preparing to teach him the real definition of the term.

148

"What," Mr. Walling growls, "are you picking on this pretty young girl for?" He shakes Ralph Edward like a woman straightening out a pillowcase before she clips it to the clothesline to dry. "You wanna be picking on someone your own size and sex." And the *s*'s hiss, steam from inner fires that repel me. *How long has Mr. Walling been watching? Has he been sitting on his porch, feet propped on the rail, nursing a beer, and watching me mow the whole yard?*

"You pretty quiet all of a sudden," he whispers to Ralph Edward. "Let go your bike, son, and let me see *your* legs, speaking of legs."

And he squeezes nerves in Ralph Edward's neck that would make a believer of him if he hadn't already confessed.

"I ain't your son," Ralph Edward spews, low and determined.

"No." And a softness comes in Mr. Walling's voice that sickens me even more. "I'm wishing you were, though, because I'd really learn you a lesson. Now drop your drawers and show this pretty girl your legs."

That does it! I let go my one connection to the earth, the lawn mower, and with both feet flying I take the yard in half a second, the front steps in another, and am screaming at McGolphin before his body is ever in sight.

"Do what?" McGolphin closes one eye and leans the other ear toward me to untangle the ribbon of

words I am reeling out. "Slow yourself, Shanta."
He places both hands on my shoulders and, frowning, listens with everything in him.

"Mr. Walling's trying to make Ralph Edward
Weathers take down his pants because he was taunt-
ing me. He thinks he's taking up for me, Mr. Walling, but I don't want him to. I can take up for myself. I hate him. Worse even than I hate Ralph
Edward."

I stop for breath and to see if McGolphin understands any of it. The silence is just long enough for
McGolphin to absorb it. Then, with a swiftness that
his sturdy frame shows no hint of holding, he's out
Louie's door to the porch, down the front steps, and
into the street where the preacher's boy still stands
astride his bike and still locked in the grasp of Mr.
Walling's huge hands.

"Is there a problem?" McGolphin asks Mr.
Walling.

I almost laugh from being winded from following
him and then hearing such an understatement of the
situation. It goes way beyond problem. *Catastrophe
is closer to the truth,* I think. Two sick minds meeting
mid-street and the bigger one going to win.

"We're handling this." Mr. Walling stalls, saying
in an unspoken way, *Leave us be to settle it ourselves.*

But McGolphin will have none of that. He
knows more of the score than he appears to.

"You know, I don't believe we've met. I'm your

150

neighbor, Finn McGolphin. Live right there across the street from you. It's a damn shame life's so busy you don't get around to meeting your new neighbors. I apologize for that."

He sticks his hand out and Mr. Walling hesitates, then takes his hand from Ralph Edward's shoulders and shakes McGolphin's hand. As soon as he does though, he loses his anger to confusion and McGolphin makes his move.

"Ralph Edward, you need to get on home now and quit making a pest out of yourself. G'wan."

Doesn't have to be told twice. He is one streak in the road.

Turning to me, McGolphin says, "Your grandmother needs you inside. I'll finish this little patch of grass for you."

I notice he doesn't say my name.

"Nice to meet you," McGolphin says over his shoulder to Mr. Walling and turns to the mowing.

I watch from deep on the porch. Mr. Walling goes inside his house and McGolphin mows.

Grandmorgan has fresh-squeezed lemonade for McGolphin when he finishes. And he finishes in the nick of time, too, because the rumbling that has been coming steadily becomes sharp thunder and it rains like an overturned bucket. The first rain Atlanta has seen in almost two weeks.

The four of us rest in Louie's room and watch the rain through the open door to the porch. Smell it as it soaks the dirt. Watch it splatter through the screen onto the tile porch floor. Watch and drink lemonade and don't talk of what happened.

When he leaves, I follow him to the front door. "Thanks, McGolphin," I say in a thin voice.

He hesitates and looks at me but doesn't say what is inside to be said. I am relieved, because I'm not sure I'm ready to discuss it yet. McGolphin just winks and leaves.

I'm eating a bowl of Cheerios when the radio blares out the news that the war is over. It's like the lifting of ominous thunderclouds. I feel a bone-deep relief.

"If I had a car," Grandmorgan bursts out, "I'd drive all through Atlanta, even over to Buckhead and Stone Mountain, and blow my horn the whole way."

People all over America are celebrating. Relief is my mode of celebration. Throw away the blackout paper. Toss the ration books. Throw out fear of bombings. Dresden won't happen in Atlanta. But then, there are different kinds of wars to consider, other ways for wars to damage.

14

Grandmorgan's hollyhocks are blooming all up and down the backyard fence. Years later I will recall only certain frames of this day and block out others. However, this is a frame I will view forever. Bees buzzing the hollyhocks and mimosa leaves fragile as small combs, tickling me high in the green of the tree. From where I am, I view back yards up and down the street. If I move one limb of the tree up, I can see McGolphin's dirt-swept back yard where his cleaning lady has scratched it with a broom. Beyond that rectangle, rests Mrs. Paige's patch of green. And houses on beyond belonging to people I've never even met.

Behind me is a field with several peach trees in

153

the middle of it. They don't bear much or well —
giving only small, hard, bitter fruit. Nobody but the
birds ever bothers with them, they are so useless.

Just by turning my head the other way I can scan
Rowena and Lelia's yard of flowers and their lit
kitchen window. Then Preacher Weathers's junky
back yard and then the back of the house on the
corner turned catty-cornered to Boulevard Drive to
address the end of the street.

This has been one of those heavy days with a hint
of cool air stirring the mimosa leaves. It's cloudy,
and twilight is quick to come. The scratch of gravel
makes me turn to look nearer home, to my own
driveway. No one appears, but I'm certain I heard
footsteps dragging small rocks across the asphalt surface. There it is again.

I climb down from the tree and, crossing the
yard, come up close to the back corner of the house
and peer around. I know. It doesn't take half an instant to put a name to the man's back sidling up
next to the rough brown stones of the house wall.
It's Mr. Walling stepping off the drive in the near
darkness and onto the soft grass border that grows
between the drive and the house. I watch as he
walks past a window and pauses to look inside, then
strolls back to the driveway until the next window
slows him down, and he leaves the asphalt to look
inside. When he reaches the front corner of the
house he strides fast on down the drive and across

the street, disappearing inside his front door. I follow at a good distance as far as the front corner of the porch to see where he goes.

I haven't seen Dennie all week. None of the Wallings. Either they've been busy deep in their house or gone. Gone, I think because the car's not there. But then you never know *who's* there and *who's* not. And that's odd because here it is Thursday night. A normal week would have held at least four or five days of time together.

I slip in the side door to our front porch. The light is off to signal any forgetful magicians that it is Thursday night. Inside Louie's partially closed door to the porch, behind its screen door, I can hear the nurse who gives him his weekly bath talking a streak. Squeeze out the washcloth into the basin. Tell Louie about her three grandchildren, humming between sentences so he can't say a word.

"Now when Harry was five, he lost his first tooth, or was he four, hm-hm-hm . . . Well, that's not important. He took up saying the most embarrassing things like . . ."

I sit in a rocker over near the front door. There is no one I can tell about Mr. Walling looking in the windows. Grandmorgan is down at Mrs. Paige's, checking to see if she has any quilt scraps that have some pink in them. I wonder if McGolphin is home. What would he do if I tell him? It would be better to catch Mr. Walling at it red-handed.

"I know one thing," I mutter to myself. "I'm going to be pulling down my shades, tight, when I go in my room next."

The nurse leaves. Grandmorgan comes back, puts out the bread money and the empty milk bottles. But I don't tell what I have seen. Just sit and rock and think about it.

"You coming to bed soon?" Grandmorgan asks as she turns to go back into the house.

"Yes'm." But I keep on rocking, watching the few stars I can see in the Atlanta sky, already bright from city lights.

I sit and think about what to do. And then, suddenly, it begins. The dog howling again . . . across the street somewhere. I stop rocking to listen to its plaintive call. I stand up and leave the porch, go down the front steps to the sidewalk. My feet are carrying me where I know I shouldn't go.

I'll get McGolphin to check it out with me, I think, and veer toward his house, climbing his steps and banging on the screen door. But as loud as I bang and call, there is no answer.

I turn and, when I come to the sidewalk again, I leave it for the curb grass and then the street and then the Wallings' curb grass and then their driveway. Mrs. Piersey's house is dark. I make sure so that the nightmare can't come true.

I walk on the grass, remembering how loud Mr.

156

Walling's footsteps were on our driveway, though it would be hard for anyone to hear me with that dog so loud. And Mr. Walling had been wearing shoes. I'm barefoot. As I pass each window I look inside for light or movement. At the back bedroom window I can see where the door opens onto the hall, so there must be a light deeper inside.

When I reach the back corner of the house, I lean against the side wall and peer around it. The back yard is empty of people. A small rectangle of light lies in the grass just in front of the stairs down to the open cellar door, and the longer I stand I become more and more certain that this is where the noise begins. I recall Honey's and my trip that day of exploring the empty house. How the cellar had left a cold distaste all through me.

Creeping through the grass, I peer into the stairwell from the side so as to avoid standing in the lighted rectangle. There is nothing in view yet, so I cross to the stair opening and go down one step, hoping to get a look at the dog. But the lower position doesn't help at all. The howling comes in waves with silences between.

When I take the next step down I realize that my shadow will show on the lighted lawn and I look back up to confirm it. Seeing it is true, I get bold and go down two more steps, and from there I see two feet on the other side of the room. Not hound paws but human bare feet. I creep down one more of the stone steps and see legs, blue-jeaned, and a bare chest.

I duck, going no farther with my feet, just with my upper body, and I see the whole person. He is familiar, even in that dim light and under those dire circumstances.

"Earl?" I whisper.

The howling stops.

"What are you doing, Earl? You sound like a dog."

He looks at me, but I can tell. He doesn't recognize me yet. He just sits, slumped against the wall.

"Earl," I whisper urgently. I make sure nobody is in the shadows of the room, then I descend the last two steps and rush to him.

"What are you doing?" I ask. "Ugh! The floor's nothing but red mud."

Earl stares at me like he's never seen me before in his life.

"Earl." I touch his hand with a patting motion I have seen my grandmother tend Honey with when she had skinned her knee.

He doesn't move.

Ha! A thought occurs. *He's being stubborn.*

"Roy," I whisper.

His eyes look at me in such an uncaring way they are two dark dots in his head, paper thin, all surface.

"It's Dale," I whisper, but know the person

hunched against the dampness of this place cares not a penny if I am Dale Evans or Joan of Arc.

My eyes take in more now. The chain from the wall is hitched through two back belt loops of Earl's jeans and locked with a padlock. He strains against it but the denim is sturdy and holds firm.

"Earl," I whisper urgently, "listen. I've been thinking about that girlfriend thing. About being your girlfriend. Remember? Maybe we could work something out. Maybe . . ."

Earl isn't in this room. He has left. Only his shell is here, and I doubt I'll be able to reach where he's gone.

The room smells worse than I recall from the time Honey and I had looked at it. It smells of urine and like somebody has thrown up. On the floor I see half a dozen beer bottles, some turned on their sides, all open and empty.

Beer? I think to myself. "Earl, you been drinking beer? What's going on? Where's Dennie?"

The name brings a flicker of recognition and he blinks and sits taller.

"Dennie!" he calls loud.

"Sh-h-h," I say, patting his hand again.

He slumps back down. "Gone," he tells me and I understand.

Overhead I hear a chair scrape the floor. *The linoleum,* I think. Isn't one of the girls. They know better. And not Mrs. Walling, as particular as she is.

Heavy treading footsteps mark the progress of a man walking. Unmistakably a man.

"I'll get McGolphin," I whisper to Earl, abandoning my first inclination, which had been to have Earl take his jeans off. Simple solution but not one Earl's mind would come up with. Too late for that now, though. "It'll be okay."

I turn and run to the stairs, but the screech of the back screen door stays me, an audible wire cutting me off. Frantic, I back against a small indented area in the shadows and cling tight as a barnacle to a ship hull.

I don't hear him come. He is just suddenly there. And I can tell by the voice it isn't Mr. Walling. It's the short, heavyset man, I guess. The uncle. I wouldn't look if money were offered.

His breathing is labored and he wheezes around a cigarette. I catch the smoke as it curls its way around the small room.

"Well, Earl, old buddy, you ready for some more beer, ain't ya! Huh? You gonna answer?"

I hear a sound like a wave meeting the shoreline and figure the man has slapped Earl. I wait for Earl's reaction, but there is none.

"Hot damn! You're learning now, Earl. When I slap you, son, it's always for your own good. Just like making you stay down to the cellar is." The man wheezes out a laugh. "You gon' do the things I ask you to do before this is all over with. You're

160

stubborn though. Stubborn, I'll tell you. You got that from your mother. Always been a stubborn woman. Always . . ."

That is when I feel something soft as a whisper brush my leg and climb my ankle. My eyes almost leave their sockets. Slowly, I take my head from the wall and lean down to look at my bare foot.

I don't care, I start telling myself, *if it's the giant of tarantulas, if it's as big as my hand, I can't move.*

My head bends farther and farther toward the floor, as I desperately try to see in the dark what something as wispy as a cobweb might be, moving along my leg.

But when my eyes find it, I jerk without control because it is the granddaddy of all centipedes. And with the jerk my clothing rubs the rock wall and makes a sound like paper moving in church.

The man shifts. I know he has heard. There is not time to decide. And anyway it's been decided for me. The noise has made the call, and all I can do is live the next moment as wisely as I know how. In one fluid movement I turn and leap up two steps, scrambling the rest of the way in desperation. He is after me with the reflexes of an athlete, economical in their directness and dead to the target. His hand catches at my foot, but I'm more desperate than he because I wrench my muddy bare foot out of his fingers and fly across the yard around the back side of the house, where the street light won't catch me.

"Hey-y-y-y!" the man roars. It sounds like he's stopping. Looking.

That is enough to rouse Mr. Walling from some room deep within the house. I hear him yelling and coming, too. But I am over behind the Warnocks' house in their tree-filled back yard by now, careful of clotheslines that can sling you back at best. Break your neck at worst.

I'm doing well, running fast until I reach the front corner of their house. There, because I'm moving so fast, I step into a hollow I can't see in the dark, a hollow where a tree once grew, and I twist my ankle good. Leaning against the house, I wince in pain. As soon as the burning joint stops consuming all of my mind, I'm able to think.

Maybe McGolphin is home. Maybe he was in the bathroom before. But how to get across the street.

I hop behind bushes and slowly look around the front corner to see if I can spot either of the men. The heavyset one is standing in his front yard one door up, scanning the street for me. My ankle hurts too bad to move fast and speed is the only way I'll get across that street.

So, I do the smartest thing I've ever done in my life. I hide up under the big magnolia tree in the Warnocks' side yard. It's so dark nobody will ever see me there and the lower branches scrape the ground. I hear the footsteps of one of the men as

162

he crosses the yard and I hold perfectly still. I will be nothing to deal with if he catches me. I know this. I wouldn't last half a minute. But he doesn't think of the magnolia tree. The feet go on by and still I wait. For the inevitable.

It isn't fifteen minutes. "Shanta! Shanta Cola! You'd better come on home now. You heah?"

My grandmother's voice is a rope to hang on to. I wait, though, for the next step. Grandmorgan will get tired of hollering out front and start worrying. Will go back inside the house. She does.

For the next part, the house could be without walls. I watch in my mind's eye. She goes through to the back porch. Then I hear her hollering out to the back yard, thinking I might be up in the mimosa tree. Coming back in, she goes to the French door in the hall, picks up the bell-like receiver hanging on the side of the telephone sitting on the hall table. Dials McGolphin's number, DEarborn 6-4289.

I give him two minutes. It is just about that long before he comes out and stands down on his front sidewalk and bellows my name a few hundred times. Then Lelia Stewart's boyfriend comes down from her front porch to see what is cooking. Now the sides are even, two against two with me as the football.

When McGolphin finally winds down and the street is quiet, I crawl out from under the magnolia tree and hop toward the street, yelling with all my might. I don't even look for the men, only McGolphin. He meets me halfway and just swings me up in his arms and carries me to my grandmother.

I don't tell them what I saw until we are safe in Louie's room, the doors shut and the window shades down tight.

15

Atlanta police come in three cars. I watch from a chair set just outside Louie's open porch door. The porch light is off and I'm soaking my foot in a basin full of warm water and Epsom salts. When the police knock at the Wallings' front door, there is no answer. No porch light comes on either. So they go around back.

"What you reckon's happening?" I say in a low voice to McGolphin, who stands just inside Louie's room so Louie won't feel left out. Grandmorgan stands pressed close to the porch screen, watching, too.

"They probably captured those fool men easy as pulling two peaches off one of your grandmother's peach trees. Probably so drunk they durn near fell in the cops' arms."

If that's so, I think, *it's taking them a pretty long time to pull two peaches.*

The Walling porch light comes on finally and an officer comes down the front steps and crosses the street to 29 Clay Street. He knocks on the balky screen door, but Grandmorgan has already moved to let him in.

"Good evening," he says, taking off his hat and wiping his forehead with his shirtsleeve. "Are you the person who called about the situation across the street?"

"Mr. McGolphin made that phone call. He's right in here."

She lets him in the living room door, completely bypassing me, stuck at the long end of the porch. They sit in Louie's room, and I feel left out now. Their low voices inside the open door are a wall that keeps me outside.

Heck, I say to myself, *short of killing him, what did they do to Earl they hadn't already done before, the other time I thought I heard the dog? And I'm the one who saw it tonight, firsthand.* It rankles me that I'm left out of the discussion.

I wait. *Surely the policeman will ask me questions. And what will I answer?* The longer I think about how I'd found Earl and all about where he was, the

166

less enthusiastic I feel about telling anybody else. Ever.

So it is a breath-releasing relief when the policeman rises to go and goes out through the living room porch door, never even looking my way.

McGolphin comes out. "How's the foot?"

I drip it up out of the now tepid water and both of us look in the dim light coming through Louie's open porch door. "Swollen."

"Sure is. Huh!" The grunt tells me swollen a lot. "Ice on it tomorrow."

I nod. "Tell me what he said."

McGolphin goes back in Louie's door, says good night, "And I need to borrow this straight-back chair for a few minutes while Shanta and I sit at this end of the porch and talk." On the porch at Louie's end, it is narrower and there is no furniture except the rocker they've dragged out there for me to sit in to soak my foot and watch. McGolphin leans his chair back until it rests against the stone house wall. Then he tells me they'd found every bit of what I'd said.

"It was a mess. How old's Earl, Shanta?"

"Twenty-one. Got a steel plate in his head, though."

McGolphin cracks his knuckles. Nods he understands the whole part of that.

Pretty soon we see four of the officers taking the men to two police cars and drive off.

"What about Earl?" I want to comfort him and take away what has happened.

"He'll be okay," McGolphin says. "He'll be coming out in a bit. The officer who came across, he said, after they washed the Georgia mud off of him, they'd take him to a hospital to be looked over and then on to a real good group home until the rest of his family comes back . . ."

"But they won't understand him there, Mc-Golphin, at the group home. He thinks he's Roy Rogers . . ."

"They been around the block a few times, Shanta. He's not the first person like that they've dealt with." McGolphin's hard voice loses no effort in attempting gentleness. His gentleness all comes from within.

"But he gets really upset if you don't call him Roy. He'll go to pieces, McGolphin, and . . ." I can't go on, it's so hard to explain.

When a few minutes pass and he can see I'm crying, he stands up. You never know with McGolphin. He might be leaving for the night. Or he might be going to fix things.

I watch him as he leaves the porch, crosses the street, and knocks on the front door. I can see the figure of the officer fill the frame and wait to hear what McGolphin has to say. They talk. Then McGolphin wheels around and comes back my way. Sits back down in the chair beside me, fishes a toothpick out of his shirt pocket, and sticks it in his mouth.

I watch him, waiting. When he is ready, he tells me. "The officer said there wasn't anybody over there name of Earl. Said his buddy was dressing Roy Rogers right that minute, while we were talking, so they can ride on out to the ranch, after they make a quick stop at the hospital."

That is when I relax for the first time in a long while.

Some people feel a person who has a steel plate in his head is less than human . . . is an animal for their pleasure. I know better though. Earl is a real person I've come to love. I'm not sure what all has happened, but I do know I'll never forget him.

16

It is a week before I see the Walling car parked in the driveway across the street. I've watched daily, but miss their arrival because of school starting and the ruckus Louray has kicked up. She had her lawyer mail a certified letter to Louie stating she is filing for an annulment of their marriage because he can no longer perform his function as a husband.

"What's his function?" I ask Grandmorgan, who just shakes her head. "Can't hold up his end of the bargain?" Grandmorgan nods.

It slowly comes to me that Louray's leaving isn't my fault after all. Nobody can blame anything but the illness and Louray's not wanting to spend her life with a man who is sick. Louie doesn't even blame her. But I do. Always.

"Will it happen? The annulment," I ask my grandmother.

"Probably. He can't go to the courthouse to defend himself. But I'll be going. You'd better believe it!"

"Will we ever see Honey again, Grandmorgan?"

"That's why I'll be going."

The court date for the hearing is set for mid-September.

"I miss them," I whisper to nobody in particular.

"I know you do," Grandmorgan says, doing the handpat for skinned knees, only this hurts harder and longer.

"You'd think," I say, warming to the subject, "if Louray ever loved Louie she'd at least bring Honey around."

Grandmorgan nods. "Love is a temperamental thing for some folks. Just as fickle as a thermometer on a spring day. Hot. Cold. Same day."

I watch the hand patting mine. The veins stand tall and blue, like long mountain ranges on the earth's surface. "You're not like that . . . are you?" I look beyond the gold-rimmed glasses, right into my grandmother's eyes.

Grandmorgan doesn't confirm or deny. She just returns my gaze and, stopping the patting, asks, "What do you think?"

171

"I think," I say, "that you won't ever stop loving me . . . or Louie . . . or Honey. Am I right?"

Grandmorgan smiles. "Yes," she says, nodding. "Love, when it's healthy, doesn't set boundaries. The bonds of love are stronger than any of us will ever know."

"Will Dennie ever see Earl again?" I ask Louie while I feed him supper. Sitting on the edge of his bed, I can see Mrs. Walling's car where it has been parked in their drive since the evening before. No one has seen them come, nor any of them since they returned.

Louie hunches his shoulders he doesn't know. "I hope so, but Mrs. Walling did leave Earl in a situation that was desperately unsafe."

I travel the distance with a spoonful of mashed, cut-up spinach and pop it into Louie's open mouth. "Maybe she couldn't help it against two strong men. Maybe she took the girls and ran for their lives."

Louie jumps on that like a duck on a June bug. "She could have gone for help."

He's right. I know it.

"Why'd those men do that, Louie? Earl hadn't done anything to them."

"I don't know. Drunk. Warped. Mean. All of the above, mostly mean. God's got a special hell for people like that . . . and that includes those animals that ran the German concentration camps, too."

I feel Louie's passion and change the subject, in a

172

way, but really lay down a thought that has a double meaning. "Well, the war's over."

Louie grunts and calms down. He takes another bite of spinach and says, after swallowing, "H-m-m-m. The bookends of a war."

I look at him. When he doesn't go further, I ask, "What?"

He smiles grimly. "Pearl Harbor. Nagasaki. Pearl, white and deadly. What's Nagasaki sound like? Jade? Onyx? A dark, stained stone. Not a real or precious jewel. Just a gemstone to make do with because it's the only way to end a war that could, otherwise, have taken a lot more lives."

I know which war Louie is speaking of. The war across the ocean. But it could just as well be the war across the street. Here in our own house with Louray. They have bookends, too, which aren't pretty, but better than no bookends at all. Only one war left for now. And it's a good one. May not be a war he'll win, but I'm betting Louie will fight his own war with disease and depression until it's over.

I scoop up mashed potatoes and feed them to him. "*Papas,*" I say.

"*Hablas español, ¿no?*" he asks with a grin.

"*Sí, hablo español.*" And when I feed him the spinach, I *show* him I can speak Spanish by saying, "*Espinacas,*" naming the vegetable.

"Good for you!" Louie congratulates me. "*¡Olé!*"

Then when I have finished the vegetables, I start

on the ice cream and know it will please him when I say, "*Helado.*"

That September Dennie and her family move away. Maybe to where they went when things got too bad, wherever that was. I suspect it is their grandmother's. I never get to say goodbye, though I mow the front grass slow and hopeful, the rest of August, once a week until school starts. At the end of the day after V–J Day, when Japan signs onto peace, the Wallings are gone. Just like that. While I was at school. Even Grandmorgan doesn't see them go. I'm sorry Dennie never got to meet Louie.

Ralph Edward Weathers doesn't pick on me anymore. One day, though, he throws rocks at my grandmother's legs as she is walking to the grocery store. Her thin, cotton-stockinged legs.

It doesn't take me two minutes to bang on Ralph Edward's front door.

"What is it?" a crack-thin voice says before the person appears. It's Mrs. Weathers.

"Your son, Ralph Edward, just threw rocks at my grandmother's legs," I say loud and firm. "And if it *ever* happens again . . . EVER . . . I'll call the police to him. One family on this street has already been arrested this summer."

I stop, realize I am trembling from the anger, but stand my ground outside the screen door. There isn't an answer given except that Mrs. Weathers shuts the wooden front door in my face.

Ralph Edward never throws another rock or bad-mouths anybody who lives at 29 Clay Street again. I figure I've told the right person.

Mr. Hadley brings Grandmorgan her half of the last batch of okra from the garden. She and I walk him out to his wagon to say goodbye until next spring.

On September twentieth Grandmorgan rises early and dresses in her Frances Virginia Tearoom dress, still snug over her girdle. She wears a black hat Mrs. Findley has given her and carries black gloves.

"You look nice, Mother," Louie tells her.

I get to stay home from school to stick with Louie while Grandmorgan goes to the courthouse to represent him in the legal situation about annulling a marriage that had begun with such love and ended in heartache.

"Well, Shanta, you take that tray on back to the kitchen when Louie finishes his breakfast now."

"I will."

"And I think I'll go ahead and walk on down to the trolley stop to make sure I get downtown on time."

"You're not due in court until ten-thirty," Louie tells her. "It's only eight-thirty now."

"I know, but I'd rather be early and relax a little."

I stand at Louie's porch door to watch Grandmorgan's hat disappear behind the althea bush as she takes the front steps sideways because of balky knees. Then she reappears again as she turns onto the sidewalk and heads for Boulevard Drive. I watch until she walks in front of Rowena and Lelia Stewart's house. Just past the chinaberry tree stands the hedge dividing the Stewarts from the Weathers and it blocks her from view.

Louie and I don't talk much that morning while I finish feeding him breakfast. In our minds we ride the trolley with Grandmorgan all the way downtown. Watch her get off. Walk to the courthouse, then climb the steep steps.

Por favor, God, I pray silently as I go sit on the front porch swing, *a courtroom is big and full of strange people. Let my grandmother do right for Louie.*

At lunchtime, when Grandmorgan hasn't returned, I fix Cream of Wheat for Louie. It's all he wants, he says. "Not very hungry."

I feed him and count the spoonfuls to occupy my mind.

About one, the mailman passes on the sidewalk, not even glancing at 29 Clay Street or me, where I've come to wait on the front porch for my grandmother.

Who'd write us? I think, and thinking it makes me feel so alone I ache. Suddenly, when I look across at Mrs. Piersey's house, I understand in an instant what the old woman has been going through.

176

During tough times, the feeling that the world doesn't care creeps in and settles on the soul. I forget the magicians that come evenings. I even forget McGolphin, who is like family. I'm on a raft in the middle of the ocean, no paddle, with nothing but sky and sun.

It is well after one o'clock when Grandmorgan comes into view. Her pace is slow but steady as she walks along the sidewalk in front of Lelia Stewart's. I jump from the porch swing to hold the door wide for her, but she turns up the driveway and comes onto the porch through the side door.

"I thank you for that," she tells me. "I just didn't think I could make it up those front steps. The gentle slope of the drive is easier to climb. I believe my feet are going to fall off at the ankles, they hurt so bad."

She passes Louie's open porch door and goes in through the living room door, calling out to him. "Be there in a minute, Hurt. Just lemme get out of these shoes."

They are the shoes she wears every day. She only has one pair. But walking the three blocks going and coming from the trolley downtown and up and down the stairs at the courthouse is so much more than her longest walks to Pannells' Grocery, two blocks over, that they have rubbed blisters.

"Whew! Would you look at that!" she says, more to herself than me. She has sat in a rocker in her bedroom to remove her stockings. "I don't know which hurts worse . . . my bones or my blisters."

"I don't see how you walked," I tell her, seeing the blisters on her toes and the backs of her heels.

"T'weren't easy."

"What if I get a basin of warm water and you soak 'em?"

"All right. Good idea. Bring it on up to Louie's room and I'll carry an old newspaper to set it on."

I move slow so as not to slosh the water. When I reach Louie's room, Grandmorgan has already told him a good deal of what happened at the court-house.

"Did she get it?" I ask after I set the tan enamel basin on the newspaper. "The annulment. Did she get it?"

"She did." Grandmorgan eases her feet into the warm water. "Ah-h-h. Stings a little but feels good."

I wait to hear more about the morning.

"Well, where was I? Oh, it didn't take the judge fifteen minutes. Said she'd heard enough. Asked me why I was there. I told her because you couldn't come . . . you didn't want to lose Honey. I said you hadn't seen her since Louray called the taxicab and left in June.

"The judge just took that in. I didn't say any more. What was there to say? She sat a minute, then said, 'That's not fair. Not right.' Those were her exact words. 'We'll fix that, Mrs. Morgan,' she says.

"Her eyes were so kind I thought she was going to have me over for coffee. She turns to Louray's attorney and says, 'I'll grant the annulment, but there's got to be some visitation privileges. No need to punish the father for something he can't help. And the grandmother.' She looks back over in my direction.

"The long and short of it is that Honey'll be coming over here one weekend a month. And if, for some reason, that doesn't happen, I'm to call the courthouse and talk directly to the judge. I've got her name and phone number written in my purse on a scrap of paper. Oh! There's something for you, too, Shanta. Honey gave it to me."

"Honey was there?"

"Yes, law! I reckon they thought they'd impress the judge by bringing Honey. She was all decked out in a little black-and-white gingham dress with a red bow at the collar. She sat right alongside Louray, still and quiet. But afterwards, she run up and hugged me, said give her daddy part of this hug, which I will soon's I get finished soaking, and she hands me a folded-over envelope. Says it's for Shanta. It's in my purse in yonder."

I find the envelope and sit in Grandmorgan's bedroom rocker to unfold it. On the outside, in uphill

179

lettering, is my name, SHANTA. I unseal it carefully and pull out a page from a school tablet, tan,
lined paper. In big, scrawling, uneasy letters, Honey
has sent her message. Her *E*'s look like centipedes,
with many horizontal lines. Three won't do her.

"Hi. I can write my name now. It's HONEY
MORGAN. Tell my daddy I love him."

I sit awhile. That alone feeling has left. My raft
has sighted land. Some weekend soon, Honey will
come and every month thereafter she will be back
for a weekend. This hurtful part of our lives with
Louray is over, but one small relic, like a live ember
shot off by a bonfire, will still warm us. Honey.

After I read Honey's note one more time, I walk
back to the front of the house to show Louie that
Honey is learning to write. To show him the words
she has written for him.

Mrs. Piersey's son comes home from the war at the
end of September, and I actually see her ride out in
a car. The spell is broken. I wave, but she's too busy
taking in the sights to notice me.

That October, a young maple tree McGolphin
had planted on the property line between our
houses turns a sudden yellow. On my walk home
from school, I can see it a block away, standing like
a lamp in the distance. Its warmth transfers itself to
the house. As I approach every afternoon, the tree

puts me in the mood for the warmth that 29 Clay Street gives off. I can feel it before I even turn into the front walk. Makes me feel like one of those Atlanta Crackers who finally gets called up to a major league team. Makes me know I belong to a family.

Betsy Manikin stands in Louie's room, watching over the house for that fall and winter and for the rest of the seven years he is to lie in the hospital bed where the magicians come to call of an evening, and where, hidden beneath the bedside table, alongside a Spanish textbook, there hangs a small cut-out picture of Charles Atlas and an awful lot of hope.

Epilogue

I mailed the letter I wrote to my grandmother on the 7th of March. Made sure the return address was there so that I'd get it back and have proof she no longer lives there. Proof that 29 Clay Street isn't her home. The red stamped hand pointing to the message that no such person lives at this address would make the truth as concrete as those gravestones out at Westview Cemetery.

It's been a year and eight weeks now since I mailed it and that letter hasn't come back yet. It could be, probably is, just lost in the mail. But I'd like to believe that somehow it reached her. And who's to say? Like she said, the bonds of love are stronger than any of us will ever know.

After I had written most of this story, I pulled an old book from a shelf one rainy fall afternoon. A small paper

*fluttered from the pages of the book and, like a winged
seed falling to the earth to grow again, landed at my feet.*
*When I opened it, I recognized the writing immedi-
ately. I also realized it was what I had been trying to say
all along.*

— S.C.M.

"I am convinced there lies within us all
the capacity to stand tall to trouble when
it comes, if the heart is willing."
— Nym Hurt

Hasta mañana, Louis. Hasta mañana.